'Goodbye,

The aggravatin[...]
shall look forw[...]

His nearness was a very real threat. Saira felt her heart beat unusually fast and was intensely aware of his raw masculinity and the danger he posed. This was no ordinary man. He appeared laid-back and friendly but beneath the surface he was as hard as steel.

Dear Reader

The nights are drawing in again . . . the perfect excuse for snuggling up with a Mills & Boon romance! November is the time for bonfires and fireworks, of course—and you'll find plenty of sparks flying between the heroes and heroines in this month's collection of love stories! Look out for books by some of your favourite authors . . . and, if you're missing the summer sun, why not let us transport you to sunny California and exotic Mexico? So shut out the winter darkness, and enter the warm and wonderful world of Mills & Boon!

The Editor

Born in the industrial heart of England, **Margaret Mayo** now lives with her husband in a pretty Staffordshire canalside village. Once a secretary, she turned her hand to writing her books both at home and in exotic locations, combining her hobby of photography with her research.

Recent titles by the same author:

DETERMINED LADY

BY
MARGARET MAYO

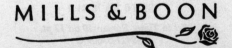

MILLS & BOON

MILLS & BOON LIMITED
ETON HOUSE, 18-24 PARADISE ROAD
RICHMOND, SURREY TW9 1SR

*MILLS & BOON and the Rose Device
are trademarks of the publisher.*

*First published in Great Britain 1994
by Mills & Boon Limited*

© Margaret Mayo 1994

*Australian copyright 1994   Philippine copyright 1994
This edition 1994*

ISBN 0 263 78741 9

*Set in Times Roman 10 on 12 pt.
01-9411-53669 C*

Made and printed in Great Britain

CHAPTER ONE

SAIRA looked forward with eager anticipation to seeing her great-aunt's cottage again—no, not Aunt Lizzie's, her own. It was hers now, she must not forget that; she was a property owner! The thought brought a smile to her face, yet it was tinged with sadness. It was going to be difficult walking into the cottage without her aunt there. Honeysuckle Cottage *was* Aunt Lizzie. The two had always been inseparable in her memory.

She could visualise the grey-stone building standing on its own at the end of the village street with its little crooked chimney and the honeysuckle after which it was named twisting and climbing all around the doorway and windows. She could almost smell the heady scent it gave off on summer evenings, and she silently urged the taxi driver to put his foot down on the accelerator.

She had happy memories of the cottage, of being spoilt and pampered and given all sorts of treats. She had been Elizabeth's favourite great-niece and had spent every summer holiday there, and many weekends in between.

Of course, when she started college she had moved in a new circle of friends and they had holidayed together, and when she qualified and got a job and her holidays were much shorter she had not visited quite so frequently. But she had always kept in touch and had worried a great deal as her aunt's bronchitis had worsened over the years.

When Lizzie had announced that she was going to spend the winter in Florida with friends, Saira had thought that, health-wise, it was the best thing she could do, and had actively encouraged her. She had never dreamt that anything would happen, had not known that her aunt had heart problems as well—she had kept that well hidden—and had been shocked to hear that she'd had a heart attack while out there and had been in Intensive Care. She had come home eventually, and everyone had thought she was adequately recovered, then she died without warning a few weeks later.

The news of Elizabeth Harwood's death had come as a considerable shock to all the family. Lizzie had been an institution, a wise old figurehead always ready to dole out advice. She had been brought home to Darlington for the funeral, buried next to her husband and other members of their family, including Saira's father.

A close solicitor friend of Elizabeth's was executor of the will and it was from him that Saira learned she was to inherit the cottage, her mother and sisters sharing whatever money there was.

As this hadn't turned out to be very much, it had seemed an unfair sort of arrangement to Saira, and she had offered to sell the cottage and share the proceeds equally. But the family knew how much Lizzie had doted on her, and vice versa, and insisted she keep her inheritance.

Both of Saira's sisters were married with homes of their own, but even at twenty-six-Saira still lived with her mother. Maybe if her father hadn't died she would have moved out and perhaps bought or rented a place—but she hadn't, and now it felt good that she owned property as well—even if she only used it for holidays. It was really too far away from her job for her to live there permanently.

The driver turned off the main road and negotiated the lanes to Amplethwaite in North Yorkshire—and to Honeysuckle Cottage. The tiny square-paned windows would probably need cleaning, Saira thought, the paintwork would be dirty, the garden might be overgrown, but it would not matter; she would soon have everything neat and tidy exactly as Lizzie had kept it.

As they reached the village Saira asked the driver to slow down, looking with new eyes at the rows of sleepy cottages, the shop, the pub, the church. It all felt different now she was no longer a visitor—it felt different too because Aunt Lizzie would no longer be there to welcome her. She would be going into an empty house, there would be no smell of freshly baked bread, no bowls of roses on the table, no cheerful greeting. A lump welled in her throat.

Saira, green-eyed and fair-skinned, had thick, dark blonde hair which she almost always wore brushed straight back off her face, plaited to one side and brought forward over her shoulder. She played with it now, as she always did in times of stress, running her fingers across the end which was like a round, fat paintbrush.

When the taxi finally pulled up she sat still for a moment surveying the silent cottage, tears in her eyes, and even after she had paid the driver and he had disappeared out of sight she still stood looking at it, and her feet were slow on the flagged path when she finally forced herself to move.

Her hesitancy turned to puzzlement and then dismay when she discovered that the key Mr Kirby had given her would not fit the lock. There had to be some mistake. Had he sent her the right one? Or——

'Excuse me, can I help?'

Saira turned at the sound of the female voice. A tiny, bent woman leaning on a walking stick, with a wrinkled face and faded blue eyes gazed enquiringly at her. 'Are you looking for someone? I'm afraid Mrs Harwood——'

'I'm Mrs Harwood's great-niece,' cut in Saira.

'You're Saira?' The old lady peered more closely and recognition dawned. 'Goodness, so you are.'

And Saira remembered Mrs Edistone too, though she hadn't seen her very often on her visits to Yorkshire. The woman had a reputation for knowing more about other people's business than they did themselves, Aunt Lizzie had used to say laughingly.

'It was sad Lizzie dying,' said the woman, her pale eyes watering.

Saira nodded, swallowing a lump in her throat. 'Indeed it was, a very great shock.'

'We all miss her. She was so well-loved in the village. What are you doing here? Have you come to sort out her things?'

'Not exactly,' admitted Saira, smiling inwardly. If Mrs Edistone wanted to know something she never hesitated to ask. 'I'm your new neighbour. Aunt Lizzie left the cottage to me.'

The older woman frowned, her pale eyes puzzled. 'But that can't be; Lizzie sold it.'

'I beg your pardon?' Saira looked at her in astonishment, a frown drawing her brows together, a faint sense of unease creeping over her.

'Lizzie sold the cottage,' the woman repeated, tapping her stick on the floor as if to emphasise her words.

Saira shook her head. 'You must be mistaken, Mrs Edistone,' she said gently. 'My aunt definitely left it to me in her will.' The woman was old; perhaps she was confusing it with some other cottage in the village.

'I'm never wrong,' returned the older lady. 'The squire bought it off her.'

'Did Aunt Lizzie tell you that herself?' asked Saira, still convinced there had to be some confusion.

'Not exactly,' she admitted, 'but I heard it from a reliable source.'

Saira had heard about Mrs Edistone's reliable sources. Her aunt used to think that the voices were inside the woman's head, that she made most of her stories up. 'Who is this squire?' she asked. 'I'll go and have a word with him.'

'Jarrett Brent,' answered her neighbour at once. 'He owns Frenton Hall. We call him the squire because he's bought up most of the property around here. Everything that goes up for sale he buys—and some that don't,' she added darkly. 'I don't know what he's trying to do— build up the estate again, I think. But those days are long since gone. I remember when——'

Saira was forced to listen to a long story about life as it used to be and it was another quarter of an hour before she could get away.

'Maybe I'll see you again?' the woman suggested pleasantly. 'You're welcome to pop in for a cup of tea any time.'

'I'll keep it in mind,' said Saira. At the moment all she wanted to do was find this man and sort the matter out without delay. Mrs Edistone was wrong, Honeysuckle Cottage did not belong to Jarrett Brent— whoever he was—it was hers, and if he dared to say differently she would fight him every inch of the way. She left her suitcase out of sight on the back doorstep and marched around the corner to Frenton Hall.

She remembered it clearly, having peered through the railings often as a child, wondering what sort of a family lived in such an enormous place; she had never seen any children and had made up stories about them being kept imprisoned by a wicked stepmother.

The Hall did not seem so intimidating as it had in years gone by; although it was indeed a huge house built of stone with long narrow windows on all sides.

In its own parkland, it was set well back from the main road, and black and gold wrought-iron gates prevented any intruders from accidentally wandering into the grounds. Saira unlatched the gates and stormed along the well maintained driveway. She was angry, very angry, more angry than she had ever been in her life. She did not take kindly to being cheated out of her inheritance by some stranger.

She stopped at the immense solid oak door and rang the bell. This man was probably taking advantage of her aunt's death. He probably assumed she had no relatives and spread the word that he had bought it. But Aunt Lizzie's will was legal and binding and if he dared to refute it she would take him to court. Already in her mind she was rehearsing what she was going to say.

The door opened and the woman who stood there looked at her questioningly, the expression on her face suggesting that she should not be there. She was tall and unhealthily thin, her grey hair fastened back in a bun. 'Yes?' The word was snapped out, making it very clear that she did not welcome uninvited callers.

'I'd like to speak to Mr Jarrett Brent,' said Saira firmly. At five feet nine and in her heels, with her head high and her eyes blazing she looked formidable, but even so she found this woman extremely intimidating. She was determined, however, to stand her ground.

'I'm afraid Mr Brent is not at home,' the woman answered haughtily, not in the least daunted by Saira's attitude. 'May I tell him who called?'

Saira groaned inwardly; she had not contemplated the possibility that he might not be in. 'When will he be back?' she asked. 'It's very important that I see him.'

'I do not know.' The woman looked at her coldly and began to shut the door.

Saira panicked and put out her hand to stop her. 'Please, I must see him today. Surely you must have some idea?'

'I expect he will be in for his lunch,' she admitted grudgingly, 'but Mr Brent never sees anyone without an appointment.'

'Then I'll make one now,' said Saira firmly. 'I'll be back at two o'clock; please make sure he knows. My name is Saira Carlton.' She turned swiftly on her heel before the woman could put her off again.

Lord, she hated the man even before she had met him. 'Mr Brent is not at home.' 'Mr Brent never sees anyone without an appointment.' The words echoed mockingly in her head. Hell, who did he think he was? He was obviously a man of some means, and he was trying to add Honeysuckle Cottage to his list of properties, but it would be over her dead body. Her aunt had wanted her to have it and no way was she going to let him trick her out of it. There was justice at stake here.

With over an hour to wait, Saira decided to have lunch in the Challoner's Arms, Amplethwaite's only pub. It was virtually empty when she first entered but the oak-beamed room was brimming with people before she had finished her plaice and chips.

She did not recognise any of them from her past visits to Amplethwaite and guessed they were all holidaymakers. She even asked the barman about Jarrett Brent, but he did not live in the village and knew very little about him. 'He never comes here. I've never seen him,' was all the answer she got.

At five minutes to two she left and at two o'clock exactly she stood on the doorstep of Frenton Hall and pressed the bell, her heart for some reason hammering uneasily. This time the door was opened straight away, the same dour woman appearing on the threshold, her face still fierce and unwelcoming. 'Mr Brent will see you,' she said, standing back for her to enter.

Saira hid her tiny smile of satisfaction. It felt like a major achievement getting past this woman. They passed through a small entrance hall into a much larger gracious hall and she looked about her with curious eyes. It was colossal, with great white columns and a three-tiered staircase and doors leading in every direction, but rather than admire it she resented the fact that this man had all this wealth while he was apparently trying to do her out of one tiny cottage.

'Through here,' muttered the woman, pushing open one of the doors.

The library was of the same immense proportions, each wall filled with books sitting in orderly fashion on glass-fronted shelves; deep, oak-framed armchairs flanked the stone fireplace, and in the hearth an arrangement of fresh roses spilled out their heady perfume. Privately she thought it a bit pretentious, all show and no warmth.

'You don't like it?'

The unexpected voice, deep-timbred and faintly condescending, made her spin on her heel and she found herself gazing into a pair of cold, intensely blue eyes. They were wide-spaced and long-lashed; in fact the man's whole face was open, as though he had a frank, honest nature, though she knew that this could not be the case.

He had a wide, generous mouth which curled upwards at the corners as if he were smiling all the time, which again was definitely wrong; it wasn't a pleasant smile, it was a mocking one. In fact his whole face was a contradiction. His eyes, though beautiful—far too beautiful for a man—were distant and assessing, his attitude faintly hostile as though he knew her reason for being here was not a friendly one.

'What makes you think that?' Saira locked her sloe-shaped green eyes into his. He was extremely tall, with a muscle-packed body and wide, broad shoulders. Normally she was as tall as most men, but not in this case, and it annoyed her that she had to look up to him.

'The way you were looking at it.' His tone was crisp and faintly defensive.

'As a matter of fact I was thinking that it didn't look lived in,' she announced coolly, then wondered at her temerity. It was wrong to rub this man up the wrong way when there was such a delicate issue at stake.

'Maybe I don't live in this particular room?' His blue eyes were watchful on hers, cool and curious, his whole stance relaxed, though Saira guessed this could be a deliberate pose, designed to put her off guard.

'But it is used?' she queried.

'Occasionally.'

'Then it would look better if a book were left out on the table, a cushion askew.' She was out of order, she knew, and it was most unlike her, but she already found this man a great source of irritation.

'Blame my housekeeper, Mrs Gibbs,' he said, his mouth curling up at the corners into a very definite smile this time, although it failed to reach his eyes; it was entirely without humour. 'She runs around after me with a dustpan and brush. One speck of dust dare not land. She's a zealot with a vacuum cleaner.'

Saira did not smile in return. Somehow she had imagined Jarrett Brent to be elderly, white-whiskered with a paunch, certainly not a devilishly handsome man in an expensive grey suit who had not yet reached his fortieth year. In fact he was probably nearer thirty than forty, possibly only a few years older than herself. The thought was disturbing. How could a man of his age have all this wealth?

'I'm not here to discuss the whims of your housekeeper,' she said shortly, wondering whether he had a wife and perhaps children, and, if so, where they were. Why this severe woman seemed to rule the roost.

'Naturally not,' he answered. 'Perhaps we should introduce ourselves? I'm——'

'Jarrett Brent,' she cut in sharply, 'yes, I know. And I'm Saira Carlton.'

He duly shook her hand and Saira was conscious of a warm, firm grip that lasted slightly longer than she liked. But if he thought he could mollify her by pretending to be friendly he was mistaken.

'Please, take a seat,' he said, gesturing towards one of the armchairs.

Saira shook her head. 'No, thanks, I prefer to stand.'

Dark brows rose. 'It's your prerogative,' and there was a distinct hardening to his tone. He clearly did not take kindly to her less than friendly attitude. 'Is there something I can do for you, Miss Carlton? Gibbs said you had an important matter to discuss.'

'That's right.' Saira drew herself up to her full height and was disappointed he still had the advantage; nevertheless her voice was firm. 'Honeysuckle Cottage.'

A frown grooved his brow, drew thick brows together, and he began to shake his head, as if he did not know what she was talking about.

'Don't tell me you've not heard of it?' Her tone was loaded with sarcasm. 'It's in the village, the first house round the corner from here. I've been told that you seem to think it belongs to you.'

His frown deepened. 'Who told you that?' he asked, a sharp, critical edge to his tone.

Saira held his eyes coldly. 'I hardly think that's relevant.'

'I do not regard my business as the affairs of others,' he told her sharply.

'What are you saying? That you bought the cottage or not?'

He appeared to consider his answer; taking a couple of paces away from her and then turning again, several seconds elapsing before he said quietly, 'I believe I did buy it.'

'*You believe*?' Saira snapped. 'Then you believe wrong, Mr Brent. The house is mine.' Her green eyes were ablaze with anger and she found it difficult to keep a limb still. This man was making fun of her.

'If you are so sure it's yours, what are you doing here?' His blue eyes were fierce also, fixed on her with unnerving accuracy.

The seemingly innocent question provoked her even more. 'Because the key I have been given won't fit. You've changed the locks, damn you. You had no right, it isn't yours. It belonged to my aunt and now——'

'Elizabeth Harwood was your aunt?' he cut in, his brows drawing together, his body growing still at this surprise information.

'That's right,' snapped Saira, 'and she——'

Again he interrupted her. 'Elizabeth and I were very good friends.'

It was Saira's turn to look astonished. 'You don't really expect me to believe that?'

He inclined his head, and now the smile was back in place. 'It's true, we had a fine friendship.'

'And you're saying you bought Honeysuckle Cottage from her?'

'That's right.' He looked supremely confident, the smile even wider now on his handsome face.

'I don't believe you.' She looked at him challengingly for several long seconds, feeling an urge to wipe the smile away; there was nothing funny at all in the situation. 'My aunt left *me* the cottage,' she blazed. 'She wouldn't have done that if she'd sold it to you.'

Thick brows rose. 'There has to be some mistake.'

'No!' Saira shook her head wildly. 'I have proof, I can show it to you.'

'I don't want to see your proof; the cottage is mine,' he announced brusquely, and again he took a couple of paces, but this time towards her.

Saira lifted her chin defensively, eyes a brilliant, angry green. 'In that case I would like to see *your* proof.'

His lips quirked. 'I dare say the deeds are filed somewhere.'

'You dare say!' stormed Saira, completely incensed by this man's far too casual attitude. 'Am I supposed to think that your word is good enough?' She had never stopped to wonder why she had not been given any deeds herself. In fact she hadn't thought about deeds at all. She suddenly realised how ignorant she was where house ownership was concerned. But she had no doubt that Mr Kirby had it all in hand.

Jarrett Brent stared at her coldly, suddenly angry. 'My word has never been questioned before.' His grey business suit did nothing to hide his masculinity; he was all raw manhood and Saira knew that in other circumstances she would have found him attractive. But not now, not today; he was the enemy and it was a serious battle she was fighting.

'Well, I'm questioning it,' Saira told him. 'I came here planning to spend the weekend and that's what I'm going to do. In fact I shan't go back home until the whole matter's sorted out.'

'There is nothing to sort out,' he announced loftily, his deep blue eyes watchful on hers. 'The property is mine and I have plans to extend and modernise it and——'

'You can't do that,' she cried out in alarm. 'It's mine. Just a minute and I'll prove it.' But a search of her handbag showed that she had forgotten to bring the letter from her aunt's solicitor.

He stood now with his arms folded across his wide chest, his legs slightly apart, his face stern, his whole stance one of haughty, powerful arrogance.

Their eyes locked and warred and Saira's chest heaved as she fought for control. He had strong capable hands, she noticed, long, well-manicured fingers spread on his forearms, and she wondered briefly what he did for a living—besides being a property owner! Power emanated from every bone in his body.

'I have proof,' she persisted, 'most definitely I have proof. I have a letter from Aunt Lizzie's solicitor. I thought I'd brought it with me, but——'

'And if I provide proof of my own?' he cut in coldly.

'I'll contest it.' Saira's voice was loud and hostile, and she tried to match his demeanour with one of her own, standing tall, her chin high, her eyes ebullient.

Jarrett Brent's lip curled, but there was undisguised admiration in his eyes. 'You're quite a spitfire.'

At his words something clicked in her subconscious, gone again instantly, forgotten in this battle of ownership. 'Aunt Lizzie wanted me to have it; we were very close. I spent all my school holidays here. She would never have sold it to you, I know she wouldn't.'

Jarrett Brent pushed his fingers through thick brown hair, cut viciously short. It would have suited him longer. The thought flashed through Saira's mind and was gone. Damn the man, what he looked like didn't matter. It was the sort of person he was that was at issue—and she sure as hell did not like what she saw.

'Perhaps she had no option?' Vivid blue eyes watched her closely.

'Perhaps you didn't give her any?' she retorted. 'Or perhaps you thought she had no relatives and decided to spread the word that you'd bought the cottage, adding it to your not inconsiderable list of properties. Oh, yes, I know all about you, Mr Brent, much more than you think.'

'Indeed?' Brows rose yet again, but there was anger now inside him. Gone was the mockery. He didn't like her attitude, the way she was sticking up for herself, the things she was saying. He had probably never met anyone like her before.

Saira knew she ought to watch herself but instead she stamped her foot. 'Lord, you're the most infuriating man I've ever met. You say *you* have proof? Well, show it to me.'

Thick brows rose reprovingly. 'Why should I do that when I have no proof that you're who you say you are? Lizzie never mentioned you to me.'

'And she never mentioned you to me,' Saira flung back.

'Then we're in a stalemate position, wouldn't you say?' Eyes locked, hostility reigned; it was a battle royal they were fighting.

'This is an intolerable situation,' she cried. 'Where the hell am I going to sleep tonight if I can't get into the cottage?'

'You could go home,' he suggested easily.

'I have no transport,' she told him, 'and even if I had I wouldn't go, not until this matter's sorted out.'

'So how did you get here?'

'I came by train and taxi,' she told him coolly.

'And you dismissed the driver without first of all making sure that you could get in?' He made it sound as though it was an incredibly stupid thing to do.

'I never dreamt for one moment that the key wouldn't fit,' answered Saira hostilely. 'Do they have rooms at the Challoner's Arms?'

'I'm afraid not.' And he looked as though the fact pleased him.

Saira eyed him stormily. 'I'll find somewhere to stay. I'm most definitely not going home until I find out who the legal owner of Honeysuckle Cottage is.' She would ring her employer and tell him that she was taking the few days' holiday he owed her.

'You're a hell of a determined lady, I'll say that for you.' It was a grudging compliment.

Saira had never needed to stand up to anyone the way she did to this man; she was seeing a new side to herself. But there was a whole lot at stake and she had the feeling that if she walked away from here now she would lose the cottage altogether. 'Where's the nearest hotel?' she asked.

'Thirsk, I expect.'

'Then perhaps you'd kindly ring for a taxi and I'll book myself in there. But I'll be back, Mr Brent, you can be sure about that.' She would phone her mother and ask her to send Mr Kirby's letter. With a bit of luck it would come in the morning and then she could present Mr High and Mighty Brent with it. That would wipe the smile off his face.

'I have a better suggestion.'

Saira frowned suspiciously. She didn't like the look in his eyes.

'You can be my guest.'

'And stay here,' she derided, 'in the camp of the enemy?' This was the last thing she had expected and it wasn't what she wanted at all. 'No, thank you.' Lord knew what his motive was, but it didn't appeal to her one little bit.

'I wasn't talking about Frenton Hall,' he answered impatiently. 'I was referring to the cottage.'

Saira frowned. 'That doesn't make sense. You're claiming it belongs to you, and yet you're prepared to let me use it. Why?'

'Just until the legalities are sorted out.' The wolfish smile on his face suggested that he knew what the outcome would be.

And although half of Saira's mind screamed that it was wrong, the other hot-headed half agreed. It was her right, after all. This thing had to be sorted out, and being here on the spot was the best way to do it. 'I guess your conscience is bothering you?'

'I was merely thinking of you,' he announced carelessly. 'It seems a bit pointless going into Thirsk when the cottage is sitting empty.' He took a key off the keyring in his pocket and handed it to her.

So the man had a heart, of sorts! Saira eyed him with no real pleasure. 'I'd like to say it's very kind of you but I don't think kindness plays a part in it. I shall be back, of course, with the necessary proof, and then you'll see for yourself that Honeysuckle Cottage is most definitely mine.'

Head high, Saira marched out into the hall and across the polished wooden floor to the door. Mrs Gibbs was nowhere in sight and when the door would not open it galled Saira to have to stand back and let the obnoxious Jarrett Brent do it for her.

'Goodbye, Miss Carlton.' The aggravating smile was on his lips. 'I shall look forward to your next visit.'

His nearness was a very real threat. Saira felt her heart beat unusually fast and was intensely aware of his raw masculinity and the danger he posed. This was no ordinary man. He appeared laid-back and friendly but beneath the surface he was as hard as steel. OK, he had offered to let her use the cottage, but she was damn sure it wasn't a simple, generous gesture. There had to be some motive.

She walked stiff-backed all the way up the long drive, wondering whether she was being watched or whether he had closed the door and immediately forgotten all about her. Meeting a man like Jarrett Brent was certainly something she had never expected when inheriting her aunt's cottage. She couldn't accept that he was a friend of Lizzie's. No friend would take your home from you. He had to be lying, and she was determined to find out the truth.

CHAPTER TWO

SAIRA felt oddly uncomfortable letting herself into Honeysuckle Cottage, and she blamed Jarrett Brent for it. He was trying it on, she felt sure, making out he had bought the cottage when really he hadn't, but he was so convincing that there had to be some thread of truth in his story. Maybe he *had* been friends with her aunt; maybe he *had* once mentioned buying her property— but Lizzie's will was surely proof enough that nothing had ever been done about it?

The front door led straight into the sitting-room and she dumped her bag and looked around, smiling sadly to herself. It was just as she remembered: a little dusty, but otherwise looking as if all her aunt had done was step out for a while.

It was a comfy, cosy room, the traditional chintz very much in evidence, lots of brass—which needed cleaning—lots of pictures and ornaments and lace mats, the usual bric-a-brac old ladies would collect over the years—and, most poignant of all, her aunt's rocking chair.

Saira felt tears spring to her eyes and her mouth twisted ruefully as memories flooded back. She had spent so many happy hours here; her aunt had read to her, played with her, loved her, kissed her better when she fell down, bathed her, fed her, brushed her hair; and as she grew older listened to her teenage problems, dispensed advice, never lectured, always understood.

Saira's own mother had always been very strict and consequently Saira had never been able to talk to her, always turning to Aunt Lizzie. She truly missed her.

But it was no good standing here crying, she must ring her mother, she must sort Jarrett Brent out. Mentally she straightened her back. To her horror the telephone line was dead, and when she tried the light switch there was no electricity either. Not altogether surprising, since the cottage had lain empty for a couple of months, but she began to wonder whether Jarrett Brent hadn't deliberately suggested she stay here knowing there were no conveniences. From what little she had seen of him so far it seemed the sort of despicable thing he would do.

Her first thought was to march back up to the Hall and confront him with it, but that was probably what he expected; he probably even hoped she would turn around and go home! It had been his cruel way of getting rid of her.

Saira's chin came up with characteristic stubbornness. She could manage for a day or two; she would light a fire to heat water, even cook that way if necessary. He would soon find she wasn't so easily put off.

Saira used the phone box at the end of the village and Margaret Carlton was equally horrified by the claims this man was making. 'Of course I'll send you the letter, but why don't you go and see Mr Kirby? Goodness, Saira, do you want me to come and sort this man out?'

Saira laughed, though there was not much mirth in her voice. 'Really, Mother, I can look after myself. I just need proof that I'm Elizabeth Harwood's niece and that I've inherited the cottage.'

Perhaps her mother was right, though, and she ought to see Mr Kirby, thought Saira as she made her way back. She glanced at her watch; almost four on a Friday afternoon—far too late. But on Monday, if nothing had been sorted out, if Jarrett Brent hadn't done the decent thing and admitted that the cottage belonged to her, she would go to see him.

She found firelighters and matches and coal and soon had flames leaping up the chimney. But her sense of achievement was short-lived when foul-smelling smoke bellowed back into the room, making her cough and choke and run to open doors and windows.

Having only ever known central heating, Saira wasn't familiar with open fires and it took her a second or two to realise that the chimney must be blocked—probably by a bird's nest.

The acrid smoke belched out ever more thickly and, not knowing what else to do Saira filled a jug with water and flung it over the coals. The joys of country living, she thought despondently. Oh, well, a sandwich and a glass of milk would have to do for her supper—if the village shop was open! Otherwise it would be another visit to the Challoner's Arms.

Fortunately the shop had not closed and Saira stocked up with a few provisions, and found out that Mrs Edistone had already spread the news that Saira Carlton was claiming Honeysuckle Cottage. 'I wish you luck,' said Mary, the elderly shopkeeper; 'the squire's not an easy man to tangle with.'

Saira spent the next hour cleaning and polishing. Little smuts of soot had settled everywhere and the smell was acrid. Aunt Lizzie had kept the place spotless and Saira wanted everything to be the same; she wanted nothing changed.

She slept that night in her aunt's spare bedroom, the one she had always used as a child, the one with rose-sprigged wallpaper and old walnut furniture, and

although she was desperately tired thoughts of the obnoxious Jarrett Brent kept her restless.

The day's totally unexpected events churned round and
round in her mind—and she still had a fight in front of
her! Something else puzzled her, too. There was something about this big man that nagged in the back of her
mind. She felt sure she had seen him some place before
but could not work out where. She tossed and turned
and thought and pondered, but no answer came.

She was up at dawn and thought longingly of a cup
of strong, hot tea, and to take her mind off it she went
for a walk. She watched the sun paint the sky with
touches of red and gold, she walked through the lanes,
she looked at Frenton Hall and called Jarrett Brent all
the names she could of, and then went back to the cottage
and ate cornflakes with cold milk.

What time did the postman come? she wondered,
sitting in her aunt's rocking chair, positioned where she
could see out of the window. Aunt Lizzie had spent hours
here watching the world go by and now Saira did the
same, rocking backwards and forwards, backwards and
forwards, her thoughts seesawing in just the same
manner, from Jarrett to her aunt, from her aunt back
to Jarrett. Could she believe that he'd had some sort of
friendship with her?

It was almost nine before she saw the familiar red post
van making its way slowly down the street and she was
outside on the doorstep when he neared Honeysuckle
Cottage. 'Saira Carlton?' he asked, and when she
nodded, 'I didn't know anyone was living here. I heard
the old lady had died. A shame, I liked her.'

'That was my aunt,' said Saira, and hoped he was not
going to stay and talk too long. She was anxious now
that she had Mr Kirby's letter to go up to the Hall and

confront Jarrett Brent. He would not expect her to get irrefutable proof quite so quickly.

To her relief the postman bade her good-day and continued on his rounds and Saira, after checking to make sure it was Mr Kirby's letter, pulled on her jacket and set off for the Hall. She kept her finger on the bellpush for several seconds and when Mrs Gibbs opened the door Saira smiled wickedly. 'I'd like to see Mr Brent, please.'

'Is he expecting you?' The same dour expression was on his housekeeper's face.

Here we go again, she thought, and tilting her chin she looked the woman in the eye. 'Oh, yes, he's expecting me all right.'

'I have not been told.'

'Nevertheless he is expecting me,' Saira insisted. Did this woman have orders or something to let no one through? 'Is he in?'

'Well, yes, but——'

'Then kindly tell him I am here.' Saira impressed even herself with her manner. It was actually quite alien for her to behave like this, but this man really rubbed her up the wrong way. She would get nowhere if she kowtowed; she had to be strong.

He was here now, walking towards the door, wearing a navy suit with a white silk shirt and a maroon spotted tie. 'What are you doing here this early?' His eyes were cool and hard and Saira resented the two steps up into the house which gave him an even bigger advantage.

She stretched herself up to her full height. 'I told you I would be back.'

'But not this soon; I wasn't expecting you today.' A frown of annoyance creased his brow.

'Well, I'm here, and I have my proof,' she told him haughtily. 'May I come in?'

'I was actually on my way out,' he announced, a touch of arrogance in his tone now. He was clearly not used to having his plans thrown into disarray—or was it hotheaded women on his doorstep who annoyed him?

'It won't take long,' said Saira, and ascended the steps before he could say another word, standing as close to him as she dared, silently demanding that he let her in, feeling the pungent smell of his aftershave assail her nostrils.

Very reluctantly he stood back for her to enter. 'I hope not.' There was extreme irritation in his voice.

'Not as far as I'm concerned,' she replied, smiling boldly.

It was not to the library he led her this morning, but a sunny breakfast room at the back of the house, the remains of his meal still sitting on the table. He saw Saira cast an inquisitive eye over it. 'Is this more to your liking? Is this lived in enough for you?' he asked sardonically.

Saira nodded. 'It's better. I take it you're not married, Mr Brent?' The question popped out without any warning and she would have liked to retract it but it was too late. In any case she wanted to know. She was curious about this man who was claiming her property.

'As a matter of fact, no,' he answered, looking surprised by her sudden question.

'And you live in this huge house by yourself?'

'For the moment, yes, but why the questions?' he asked with a frown. 'I thought you were here to discuss Honeysuckle Cottage.'

'Yes, I am,' she returned sharply, annoyed by her own digression. His marital status was of no importance whatsoever. She delved into her bag. 'I have here the letter from Mr Kirby, my aunt's solicitor. Please read it.'

His fingers brushed hers as he took the single sheet of paper and Saira jerked away, unable to make up her mind whether his touch was deliberate or accidental. Whatever, it had a profound effect on her, almost as though she had been burnt. It was an astonishing feeling.

And if the touch had been deliberate, what did it mean? Had he realised that he was up against a tough woman, someone who would not easily relinquish her hold on the cottage, and thought he would appeal to the feminine side of her? Or was she letting her imagination run riot?

Saira squashed the traitorous thoughts immediately, watching Jarrett Brent as he read Mr Kirby's letter, shocked beyond belief when he thrust it dismissively back into her hand.

'This doesn't mean a thing,' he said harshly.

'What do you mean, it doesn't mean a thing?' cried Saira, unable to accept that he was dismissing it out of hand. 'Of course it means something; it means the cottage is mine!' She was really uptight now; she had been so sure that this was indisputable proof.

'And how can that be when I say *I* own it?' Profound blue eyes held her trapped like a deer in a car's headlights.

'Prove it,' she said furiously.

There was a sudden gleam in his eyes and his lips curved into their usual contemptuous smile.

Saira fumed. He was so damn sure of himself. Could he possibly be right? Maybe she ought to have spoken to Mr Kirby first, brought him with her perhaps? She was too impetuous for her own good. She had the feeling that she was getting deeper and deeper into this thing instead of being somewhere near solving it.

'I can't at this moment, I'm afraid.' His eyes pierced hers with an intensity that was intended to put her down, his tone in no way apologetic.

'I bet you can't,' she snapped, prepared to wager her last penny that he just didn't want to admit that he was in the wrong. Either that or he was playing some game with her, though for the life of her she could not think why.

'But I've no doubt I'll come across the relevant documents,' he added.

'I'm sure you will—when it suits you.' Saira's tone dripped sarcasm. 'And meantime I'm left in a state of limbo. That is not satisfactory, Mr Brent.'

His lips quirked, as though he was enjoying her high dudgeon. 'It is the best I can offer.'

'And how long do you intend to keep me waiting?' Saira felt an electric tension crackling between them. Lord, she hated this man; was there ever anyone more disagreeable? Why was he acting like this? What was he hoping to gain?

'Is there any rush, Miss Carlton?' Cool eyes never wavered; they pierced her with an intentness that was extremely disconcerting. She had never felt more at a disadvantage.

But her chin was high as she answered. 'As far as I'm concerned, there is. I'd like to settle this matter as soon as possible. I don't like being kept dangling like a fish on a hook.' He was probably expecting her to complain about the lack of amenities in the cottage, but she was damned if she would. There was no way she was going to let this man get the better of her.

He smiled suddenly, surprisingly, a wide smile that softened the harsh lines on his face. 'A very beautiful fish.' But his narrowed eyes were unreadable. 'I'll do my best, that's all I can say.'

Saira dismissed his flattery out of hand. 'This doesn't mean a thing to you, does it?' she flared. 'You don't understand or care that to me it is very important. A cottage is a cottage as far as you're concerned, bricks and mortar with no sentimental value. You'll do whatever you want without a thought that it was my aunt's home for most of her life, tended lovingly, and then left to me so that I could give it the same thoughtful care.'

'As I said before, your aunt never mentioned you,' he reminded her.

Saira lifted her shoulders. 'That doesn't mean a thing. There was no reason for her to. And it's my aunt's property we're discussing, not my aunt or my relationship with her.

'*My* property,' he amended, and the smile was gone as swiftly as it had appeared.

'*If* you bought it, then you some way swindled her out of it,' she cried recklessly. 'I shall get to the bottom of this, Mr Brent, you can be sure. I shall expect proof from you tomorrow; I want you to bring the deeds to me and show me that the cottage is really yours, and if I don't get proof then I shall go and see Mr Kirby.'

'You're a hell of a fiery lady, Miss Carlton.' There was once more grudging admiration in his voice.

'I guess I have to be with someone like you,' she riposted. There was no way she could meekly accept his word. She was fighting as much for Aunt Lizzie's sake as her own.

'Someone like me?' he pondered, an eyebrow quirking. 'I'd be interested to hear exactly what you do think of me.'

'Oh, I don't think you would,' retorted Saira with a half-laugh. 'It wouldn't be fit language for a lady.'

'That bad, huh?'

'That bad,' she agreed. 'You're the most obnoxious person I've ever met.'

'And all because your aunt sold me the cottage?' Brows rose, blue eyes challenged and Saira felt a strong, deliberate, sexual challenge as well. It was nothing she could put her finger on, it was just there, hanging in the air between them.

Nor could she deny it. Her heart hammered and she licked suddenly dry lips; her heart went boom and her skin grew warm. 'All because *you say* Aunt Lizzie sold it,' she retorted. 'Personally, I do not believe you, and the fact that you haven't produced any proof is surely evidence enough? What reason would you have for holding back on it?'

'I never do anything without a reason, Miss Carlton.'

Her eyes flashed. 'But you're not going to tell me what it is? You're playing some sort of game that only you understand?'

'You could be right,' he answered easily.

'Of course I'm damn well right,' she snapped. 'Lord, you take some understanding. It's no wonder you've never married; no woman would ever put up with you.'

His smile faded. 'My bachelor state is of my own choice,' he told her coldly. 'How about you, Miss Carlton? No ring on your finger either, I see. Am I right in suspecting that it's your prickly nature that puts men off?'

Saira drew in a deeply aggrieved breath. 'For your information, Mr Brent, I'm not usually so abrasive.'

'So it's me who rubs you up the wrong way?'

'That's right.'

'It need not be,' he told her calmly. 'If you'd only accept that your aunt——'

'Never!' cut in Saira fiercely. 'A legal document is surely more binding than your word?'

He laughed. 'But you're forgetting, I haven't seen a legal document, just some letter, not your aunt's will. Anyone could have written that. You could have done it yourself for all I know.'

'Then I suggest you ring Mr Kirby and verify it,' she blazed.

'Maybe I will on Monday,' he agreed, much to her surprise. 'Meantime, enjoy your stay in the cottage.'

'Meantime, I want *your* proof tomorrow,' she slammed back, and then turned and marched out of the house.

As she walked back down the drive she felt as limp and washed out as if she had been put through an old-fashioned mangle. It was difficult to believe how arguing with this man could drain her so much. God, he was detestable. He was virtually laughing in her face and she was expected to sit back and take it. Not on her life. This would probably be the strongest battle she would ever fight—but she was determined to win.

The day dragged interminably slowly. There was not much she could do without a car. Trust her old Fiesta to break down at a time like this—not that she would have trusted it to make the journey here. She really ought to invest in a new car. And if she had still been going out with Tony he would have brought her. Everything, but everything, was conspiring against her.

Tony had been her boyfriend for two years and she really had thought they would get married as soon as he'd finished law school and found himself a job. Originally he had trained in the police force but had then decided it was not for him, so even though he was twenty-seven he was a student and not earning any money.

When he had declared only two weeks ago that he thought their relationship was getting nowhere and they ought to part, she hadn't been able to believe it. She had never minded that they couldn't very often afford to go out. It wasn't until one of her friends told her that she had seen him with another girl that it all became clear. The break-up had left her very bitter. If he'd had the guts to tell her that there was someone else she would have thought more of him.

He wasn't the only man to two-time his girlfriend, either. She'd had friends who'd been let down in a similar manner and it left her with a very bad taste in her mouth as far as the whole male race was concerned.

She ate again at the Challoner's Arms, took a stroll through the lanes, and went to bed early. How long Jarrett Brent was going to keep her waiting, she didn't know. Would he come tomorrow with proof or would it be up to her to go and see Mr Kirby?

On Sunday morning the church bells were ringing and Saira decided to go to morning service. She had always attended with her aunt and it felt only right that she should do so now.

The small church, its pews each with their own individual doors, was almost full, and many eyes turned in her direction. Some people smiled, some were openly curious, and Saira had no doubt that they all knew who she was.

The young vicar's sermon was amusing yet moral and Saira began to feel uplifted, until she turned to leave and saw Jarrett Brent a few rows behind her. Their eyes met, he smiled, briefly, perfunctorily, and then turned his attention to the girl at his side.

She was small, dark and fragile-looking, with a classic bone-structure—and she was wearing a hat! The only young woman to do so. It suited her without a doubt, she looked stylish and elegant, and Saira felt immature and gauche in her cotton dress and jacket, her hair in its usual plait.

So Jarrett did have a girlfriend after all! Was it serious? He had said he lived on his own *for the moment*. Perhaps they were planning to get married? The girl was gazing adoringly at him, it was obvious they had a very deep relationship.

Deliberately she hung back until he had gone. She wouldn't have said that this girl was his type, she looked very fragile and meek, not as though she could stand up to a man like Jarrett Brent. Or was that the type he preferred? Did he like to boss his women around? And why was she wondering about it? What did it matter to her?

Mrs Edistone appeared at her side while she was still deep in thought. 'Good morning, Saira. I see you got in, then?'

Saira nodded and smiled. She had seen the woman's curtains twitch several times and knew that her comings and goings had been carefully monitored.

'The squire gave you a key?' asked the old lady, leaning on her stick, looking as though she was prepared to talk for a long time.

'Yes,' answered Saira.

'I suppose he's not a bad man,' Mrs Edistone reflected thoughtfully, 'always very pleasant if you meet him in the street, very pleasant indeed, very pleasant. How did he seem to you?'

'Very pleasant,' repeated Saira seriously, while inside she was dying to laugh. 'Very pleasant' were the last words she would use to describe Jarrett Brent. Very disagreeable, very uncooperative, very everything else, but 'very pleasant'? Not on your life.

Saira had a ham sandwich and salad for her lunch and when two o'clock came and went and he had still not brought her the requested proof she decided to go up to the house again. She refused to sit around all day waiting.

As she walked up the long drive Saira wondered whether the pretty girl would be there? Or indeed whether her antagonist would be in? It was feasible that he had taken his girl out to lunch and they might not be back yet, perhaps this was why he had not come. But she had no doubt that Mrs Dour, as she had nicknamed his housekeeper, would put her in the picture; she would probably take great pleasure in turning her away.

To Saira's amazement she felt her heart beating much faster than normal, and she took a few deep breaths to calm herself as she pushed the bell and waited. It was a long time before anyone came, she had rung again and was on the verge of leaving when the heavy oak door swung inwards and Jarrett Brent himself appeared. 'Oh, it's you,' was his greeting, and he looked irritated at being disturbed.

'Yes, it's me,' confirmed Saira loudly and aggressively. 'I've been waiting for those papers. Have you found them yet?'

'Actually, no.' The annoying sardonic smile was in place, his true feelings well hidden.

Her eyes flashed. 'I bet you haven't even looked.'

'I have been rather busy,' he admitted.

And Saira knew who he was busy with right now. His shirt was unbuttoned, his hair tousled; he looked as though he had dressed in a hurry.

'Let's get one thing quite clear,' she said fiercely, 'I'm not moving off this doorstep until I get what I came for.' She planted her feet firmly on the ground, stood tall, and looked him full in the eyes.

His lips quirked. 'That could prove extremely uncomfortable, because I've just remembered that the papers in question might be in my office safe and not here. I'm afraid I can do nothing about it until tomorrow.'

'*Might* be in your office safe?' she questioned in disbelief, her voice rising as her temper increased. 'You mean you're not sure?' It was unbelievable.

'I'm as sure as I can reasonably be.'

'I think you're lying,' she spat. In fact she was absolutely sure he was lying. 'I think that for reasons known only to yourself you're keeping me waiting. I think you're devious and conniving and I cannot think what my aunt saw in you.'

He lifted his shoulders, still with that infuriating smile on his face, not at all perturbed by her outburst. 'You're at liberty to think what you like.'

Saira stamped her foot. 'Lord, you're impossible. This is a most intolerable situation.'

'Actually I'm rather enjoying it.' The smile turned to a grin.

'You would,' she returned sharply, hating the way he was so in control of himself while she was in danger of losing her composure altogether. 'I'm the one who's being messed around. *If* the papers are in your office safe, and I don't believe for one second that they are, why couldn't you have told me that in the beginning?'

'Because it wouldn't have been half so much fun,' he admitted. 'Are you always this fierce and fiery, this impatient?'

Saira could see nothing funny at all in the situation and she glared, her green eyes flashing like jewels. 'Impatient? I'm not impatient, I'm just anxious to set the matter straight. You're procrastinating deliberately and I demand that you go and find your deeds right now this very minute. Either that or tell me the truth—that you don't own Honeysuckle Cottage.'

'Why don't you believe me, Saira?' His own patience suddenly snapped, his mouth tightening, his eyes growing hard; but his voice was soft, and all the more menacing because of it. Saira felt the unspoken threat.

'Give me a good reason why I should.' She glared belligerently and drew herself up to her full height, which was still nowhere near tall enough to meet his eyes on the same level, especially with two steps between them. Saira fumed. She felt so impotent; he was playing with her like a cat with a mouse and she was unable to do anything about it.

'My word is not usually doubted.' He spoke the words easily but his arrogance showed through, incensing Saira even further.

'I'm doubting it now,' she flung savagely. 'You've fobbed me off for long enough. I refuse to move until you go and find those deeds.'

'Darling, who is it?' A gentle voice came from behind Jarrett and as he turned Saira saw his female friend. The girl looked calm and self-assured and there was no sign that she and Jarrett had been making love a few minutes earlier. But Saira was not fooled; she had had plenty of time to tidy and compose herself.

'Joy, come along and meet Miss Carlton.' He brought the other girl forward into the doorway, and when he took her hand Saira felt a stab of impatience. Here he was, playing around with this girl when there were far more important matters at issue.

The dark-haired girl, who looked impossibly delicate, smiled and eyed Saira curiously.

'Joy, this is Saira Carlton, Lizzie's great-niece; you remember Lizzie, don't you? And Saira, I'd like you to meet Joy Woodstock.'

The two girls shook hands and Saira noticed that he hadn't actually said who Joy was. A deliberate omission, she felt sure. He wanted to keep her guessing; it was all part of the game he was playing. Despite having met him two or three times now, she still knew nothing at all about him—*nothing except that he was claiming her inheritance*!

'Why don't you ask Saira in, darling, instead of keeping her standing here on the doorstep?' The fact that the girl showed no curiosity proved to Saira that he had already discussed her, that she probably knew every detail, knew he was playing some dishonourable game with her where Honeysuckle Cottage was concerned.

'Would you like to come in?' he asked with exaggerated politeness and a twinkle in his eye, because he knew perfectly well that she would refuse.

'Would it be worth my while?' she asked, chin high, eyes challenging.

'If you're asking whether I will produce the evidence you require, then the answer is no; but if you'd like to join Joy and me for a cup of tea, then you're welcome.' His eyes dared her to accept and Saira almost agreed— except that she would be hurting no one but herself. Did she really want to sit and see these two making eyes at each other? The answer had to be no.

This man sickened her—although she could not deny his overt sexuality. Her awareness of it increased each time they met—and it was a source of great annoyance. She was not interested in this side of him, not one little bit; Joy was welcome to his body and his bed.

'Thank you for your offer, but no,' she said with careful politeness. 'I came here for one thing only and as it's not forthcoming I will return to my aunt's cottage. But, Mr Brent, my patience is not without its limits. Please make sure that you have the necessary papers available for me tomorrow.'

It was an unnecessary speech, but she felt better for it, and without even waiting for his answer, catching only a glimpse of Joy's surprise, she spun on her heel and headed swiftly back towards the cottage.

I seem to be spending all of my time walking up and down this drive, she thought humourlessly. There was no end to her torment. This man really was taking a great deal of pleasure out of her helplessness. And most definitely she would get in touch with Mr Kirby in the morning, whether Jarrett Brent came up with proof or not. It would still only be his word. She had to make very sure of her legal position before giving anything up to him.

CHAPTER THREE

THAT night Saira dreamt about Jarrett, a vivid, disturbing dream where he came to the cottage in the middle of the night and made love to her. To begin with she had fought him, fought desperately to keep him away, but he had worn down her resistance and she had given in, and her body had experienced such feelings of intense pleasure that when she awoke they still persisted.

For a few moments she remained curled in a cocoon of mystic warmth and happiness, hugging the feelings to her, and then the realisation of what she was nurturing hit her like a body blow and she sprang out of bed absolutely disgusted with herself.

This man was her enemy, for goodness' sake—and yet the pleasure had been so real it was unnerving. She could remember it as clearly as if it had actually happened—and she had to face him today! Her cheeks burned at the thought and her only saviour was that he would not know what was going on in her mind.

The dream, and the feelings that went with it, were even more amazing considering the way she felt about men at this particular stage in her life. Tony had done such a good job of hurting her that she did not want to enter into a relationship with any other man for a very long time, perhaps ever.

Even the fact that she had let Jarrett make love to her in her dream went against all the principles she had ever held. She did not believe in sex before marriage. Both of her sisters had got pregnant before they were married and she was determined it was not going to happen to her.

Tony had accepted her wishes without question and, looking back now, it was obvious that he had never truly been in love with her, and there had definitely never been any explosion of feeling between them such as she had experienced in her dream. That had been unreal, like the stuff you read about in romantic novels.

She would have loved to shower now and rid herself of the feel of Jarrett from her body. Not that her aunt had a shower anyway, but she could have bathed—if there had been hot water! Everything was conspiring against her—and she blamed Jarrett Brent totally; he was the instigator of all this.

She couldn't and wouldn't accept that her aunt had sold out to him. He was taking advantage of the situation, he was trying to swindle her out of her rightful inheritance. He wanted the cottage, he wanted to do it up and possibly sell at a profit, and he was prepared to go to any lengths to get it.

After washing in cold water and dressing in a pair of jeans and a yellow T-shirt, Saira ate her now usual breakfast of cornflakes, tidied the kitchen and cleaned the bathroom, and still it was too early to ring Mr Kirby. She went into the village and took some photographs; of the cottage, of the village street, of the church, of all things to remind her of Amplethwaite, everything except Frenton Hall!

It puzzled her that Jarrett Brent lived alone in such a huge place. Was it a family home? Had he lived there all his life? She could not remember hearing the name Brent before, but maybe it was that she hadn't listened, hadn't taken it in when she was a child.

Soon after nine she phoned Mr Kirby's office, only to be told, much to her disappointment, that he was out visiting a client. 'Can I get Mr Kirby to ring you?' asked his secretary.

'I'm afraid that's not possible,' Saira answered. 'I'll call back this afternoon.' She had not expected this, not first thing on a Monday morning, and she fumed impatiently as she made her way back to the cottage.

At one she made herself a cheese sandwich and at half-past Jarrett Brent knocked on the door. Saira felt a deep depression settle over her. There could only be one reason for his visit—he had come to gloat, he had brought the necessary proof that he owned the cottage!

It was a disquieting, disturbing thought, because although she had asked for it, she had not really expected it, or wanted it even, but as she opened the door and saw him standing there in a pair of beige linen trousers and a darker brown polo shirt, all thoughts of deeds fled. Saira relived again her vivid dream and felt an impossible heat pervade her body, even her heart clamoured and she thanked God he couldn't see the turmoil inside her.

She saw him in a different light today, she saw not her enemy but a sexually attractive man who had the power to bring her whole body to such fever pitch that it was frightening. OK, it had all been a dream, but the feelings were still there and they scared her to death and her eyes were wide as she looked at him.

His brows rose in a crooked line. 'You're looking at me as though I'm a ghost or something. Is there anything wrong, Miss Carlton?'

She swallowed hard and pulled herself together, his formal use of her name helping to rationalise her feelings, to put a certain amount of space between them. It allowed for no intimacies and she liked that, she wanted to forget the all too real feel of his body against hers in the dream. He was a hard-muscled man and yet his skin had been smooth, only faintly covered with hair, nothing rough, nothing to put a barrier between their two bodies.

She found herself wondering whether he really was like that and then shook her head angrily. 'I suppose you'd better come in,' she invited with reluctance, 'but actually I was wondering why you're empty-handed, why I get the impression that you don't come with good news?' She deliberately made her tone sharp.

His eyes narrowed. 'On the attack already?' But his voice was cold too and Saira knew this wasn't going to be a pleasant meeting.

'It's pretty obvious I'll be angry when you're messing me around like this,' she retorted. 'I don't like being kept waiting. If you can't provide proof then why don't you admit it? Please sit down.'

'There's been a hold-up,' he told her, dropping into her aunt's rocking chair, completely relaxed, his long legs stretched out in front of him, his hands linked behind his head, his eyes watchful on hers.

Saira's chin lifted fractionally as she perched herself on the edge of a chair opposite, and her fingers curled. She was ready to do battle. 'Really?'

'Yes, really. My estate manager has been taken ill and I have no idea where to look in his highly personalised filing system.' He looked at her levelly as he spoke, but a sudden quiver to his lips made her suspicious.

'You said they were in *your* safe,' she reminded him.

He lifted his shoulders. 'Mine, my estate manager's—what difference does it make?'

She eyed him furiously. 'A hell of a lot. Why don't you quit stalling and tell me the truth?'

'Come, come, Miss Carlton, losing your temper will get you nowhere.' He was almost smiling but not quite; it was just his lips that curled.

Blue eyes met green and Saira was the first to look away. It was unreal how one single dream could have such a devastating effect. She hated this man and yet felt such a strong physical awareness that it almost took her breath away. 'Doesn't your estate manager have a secretary?' she asked, trying to keep her voice cold, not wanting to give him the merest hint of the turmoil inside her.

'I'm afraid not.' His answer was delivered so easily, so perfunctorily, that she knew he was lying, yet she knew equally as strongly that he would never admit it.

'So what are you suggesting?' How she wished she were a man so that she could take a swipe at him. She needed to do something, she needed to get him out of her system, he really was the most aggravating man she had ever met.

'You could go home, leaving me your address, and I'll get in touch with you eventually.' He was still totally relaxed, totally in control; they could have been discussing the weather, or something equally uninteresting, certainly not the major issue of Honeysuckle Cottage.

Saira felt incensed and bounced to her feet. 'No, most definitely not. I categorically refuse.' Lord, what did he take her for, a fool?

'What, to give me your address?' He made no effort to move himself, looking up at her with that irritating smile that made her want to lash out at him.

She shook her head, pigtail flying. 'To go away without getting what I want. Hell, will you stop playing games with me?' Never in her life had she been so angry so often. She was not usually a volatile person. This man rubbed her up the wrong way—and she felt sure he was doing it deliberately, that he took great pleasure out of goading her, though for what reason she had no idea.

'Games?' His brows rose as though he wondered how she could possibly think such a thing. 'I'm perfectly serious, lady. But it's your prerogative to do whatever you wish.'

Saira glared. 'I don't care about prerogatives, I care about justice. You're stringing me along, aren't you? You're not producing the deeds because you don't possess them, although for reasons known only to yourself you're letting me believe that you can't lay your hands on them.'

She paused and drew in a deep breath. 'But if you want to play dirty we'll see what my aunt's solicitor has to say when I get in touch with him later. Maybe he has the deeds, I don't know, I never asked him, but I'll find out, you'll see, and then I shall expect an apology, a big one.'

Finally he rose to his feet but he was completely unperturbed by her outburst; in fact he was highly amused, his smile wide, his teeth very white and slightly uneven.

'You needn't look so happy,' she cried, her chest heaving, her eyes over-bright, 'I mean it. I've had enough of your procrastination.'

Jarrett Brent shook his head slowly, his blue eyes steady on her face, the smile still there. 'You're quite a woman, Miss Carlton.' And he took a step closer.

Saira stepped back in panic, remembering her dream, aware that it would be all too easy to become intoxicated by his raw, sensual maleness.

'I've never met such a wildcat before.' His voice went a note lower.

'You wouldn't have done so on this occasion if you hadn't treated me so badly,' she returned sharply, defensively, her heart beginning to pound.

'I'm not complaining,' he assured her. 'You have a healthy temper and I admire it. I like a woman who sticks up for her rights.'

'How can you possibly like me, Mr Brent, when I'm the enemy?' She kept her tone hard, it was imperative she did not let her anger slip.

'Enemy?' His brows lifted. 'I don't see you in that light. A firebrand, a spitfire, a woman intent on fairness, but not my enemy, no. And don't you think it's about time we dropped the formalities?' His voice deepened even further. 'My name's Jarrett. I'd like you to use it.' Again he took a step closer and now there was only inches between them.

The way he was behaving, Saira could see her dream becoming reality, and if he should dare to touch her she would be unable to resist him; the barriers had already been dealt with. It was stupid to give such importance to a dream but she could not help it; it had been so real, *was* so real.

Again she shook her head firmly. 'I prefer to be formal. It's pure business between us, and once the matter of the cottage is sorted we shan't see each other again.' She kept her chin high, her back straight.

'That would be a pity,' he said quietly. 'I'm beginning to quite enjoy our exchanges.'

The mockery in his voice incensed her. 'I'm afraid I can't say the same,' she tossed coolly. 'I've had a disastrous weekend and now I'm having to take time off work just because you can't be bothered to sort out a few papers.' She took a step away from him. 'I need a shower and to wash my hair, I'd like to be able to cook a hot meal and make a cup of tea, and the longer you keep me waiting the more desperate I'm becoming.' The moment the words were out she regretted them; she had had no intention of letting him know that the lack of amenities bothered her.

'Ah!' It was an exclamation of triumph. 'I wondered when we'd get to that. Do you know, you've amazed me? I know of no other woman who would have put up without mod cons for so long. How long are you prepared to live this way? Or will you go home once you've been to see Lizzie's solicitor?'

'Only if the matter's sorted out,' she declared. 'I've decided I shall stay here as long as it takes.' It was a spur-of-the-moment decision but she hated the thought of this man winning. It had become a real issue with her.

Blue eyes glinted. 'You're a hell of a determined lady.'

This was the second time he had said that but she wasn't flattered. 'I don't like being taken for granted,' she snapped. 'You thought I'd accept your word that this cottage is yours, didn't you? You thought I'd turn around and go away again? Well, I won't, I tell you; I'll fight it out to the bitter end.' She paused and looked at him, frowning. 'Haven't I met you somewhere before, Mr Brent?' The notion had returned again suddenly and quite strongly.

'No, I don't think so,' he said with some surprise. 'I'm sure if I'd met someone as lovely as you I would never forget.'

Saira shook her head dismissively. 'You seem familiar. I thought it the first time we met and the more I see you the more convinced I am.'

His lips twisted wryly. 'I'm afraid you have the wrong person, more's the pity.'

'Have you ever been to Darlington?'

'Many times,' he affirmed, 'especially to see Stephenson's *Locomotion*. I have to admit I'm a bit of a railway buff. Is that where you live?'

Saira nodded. 'What do you do for a living?'

He frowned. 'What is this, an inquisition?'

She shook her head. 'It doesn't matter, I'm not really interested.' She looked at her watch. 'It's time I phoned Mr Kirby. Are you going?'

Her bluntness caused a wry twist of his lips. 'Am I being thrown out?'

'As we have nothing further to discuss, yes.' She crossed the room and they reached the doorway together. She thought he would stand back and let her through but he didn't and their bodies brushed as they both moved at the same time. Lord, it was like a replay of her dream. Senses awoke, nerve-ends quivered, her heart panicked.

When his arms steadied her, when she felt herself crushed against a rock-hard body—a body she had felt before!—Saira began to suspect that it hadn't been accidental. Her protest was loud and swift. 'What are you——?'

His mouth cut her off in mid-sentence, his lips assaulting hers, a kiss designed to arouse, to let her see that there could be more between them than enmity—if she allowed it! She had allowed it once, or so it seemed, but not again; no, not again. It was indecent, this response she had to him, it was foolish and fatal and yet— she hadn't the strength to push him away.

The kiss was everything she remembered, shockingly exciting, stunning her, appalling her, and she pushed and struggled and finally managed to free herself. 'How dare

you?' she cried. 'You bastard! Keep away from me or
I'll have you arrested for assault.'

He grinned, looking very complacent. 'One kiss hardly
constitutes assault.'

'It does when it's not welcome. Get out of here this
minute.' She was all the more angry because of her
response.

'Don't you think you're over-reacting?'

'No, I do not. You had no right kissing me.'

'Why, when there's no other man in your life? There
isn't anyone, is there?'

'As a matter of fact, no,' she answered sharply, 'but
that isn't the point. I don't want that sort of a relationship with you.'

'Is it because of Joy?' A light gleamed in his eyes. 'A
sense of propriety because you think I'm already spoken
for?'

'Of course not,' she snapped. 'Although I feel sorry
for her if this is the way you behave behind her back.
You men are unbelievable. You're so smooth, so arrogant, so completely sure that we women will fall at
your feet.'

'Not you, Saira,' he admitted grudgingly. 'You're quite
something. But I will go, if you insist; I'll let you make
your phone call—but perhaps later I could take you out
for dinner?'

The nerve of the man! Saira shook her head in astonished disbelief. 'Because you feel sorry for me?
Because it will ease your conscience? Because I didn't
react as you thought I would when you *magnanimously*
let me stay in this cottage?' she asked savagely. 'No
thanks.'

There was a pause, a moment when a mixture of unreadable emotions crossed his face, then he said decis-

ively, 'I will not take no for an answer; I shall pick you up at seven-thirty; please be ready.'

Before she could speak again the door closed behind him and Saira was left feeling thoroughly unsettled. First the dream, then the kiss, now a date—what else was going to happen? What more was he expecting? And when was he going to settle the matter of the cottage?

Saira's phone call to Mr Kirby was thoroughly unsatisfactory. 'Elizabeth always kept the deeds in the house,' he explained. 'I often told her it was a mistake, that she ought to have all her valuables locked away, but she wouldn't listen. I intended to ask you to find them out so that everything can be changed into your name.'

'I see,' said Saira slowly, and hope began to dawn. If she could find them... 'Has she ever spoken to you about a Mr Jarrett Brent?'

'No, I don't think so,' he said slowly, thoughtfully. 'Who is he?'

'He's a neighbour and he's claiming the cottage is his,' Saira told him tersely. 'He says my aunt sold to him.'

There was a long pause at the other end. 'Are you sure?'

'Yes, of course I'm sure,' she said, trying her hardest to hide her impatience. 'He's making my life a misery.'

'Elizabeth never said anything to me about it. Does he have any proof?'

'He claims to possess the deeds,' said Saira, her voice loaded with sarcasm, 'but in three days he's failed to come up with them. I'm glad I've spoken to you; I'll go right back now and have a good look.'

'This is most irregular,' said Mr Kirby and she could hear the worry in his voice. 'Let me know if you come across anything, and meantime I'll send Mr Brent a letter. Do you have his address?'

Back at Honeysuckle Cottage Saira painstakingly went through every drawer and cupboard, through her aunt's old handbags, coat pockets, everything. To begin with her hopes were high; she felt sure she would find the deeds and she would have great pleasure in waving them in front of smarmy Jarrett Brent's face.

But her spirits fell as her search revealed nothing. There were all sorts of papers in a tin box; old letters, receipts, theatre tickets—but no deeds. Neither was there anything to say that her aunt had sold the house to Jarrett Brent! That had to mean something.

When she had finished, when she had finally given up, Saira caught sight of herself in the mirror in her aunt's bedroom and was amazed to see how dusty she had got. What she needed was a hot bath! She sighed at the thought of such luxury, and knew cold would have to do. Thank goodness it was summer.

But before she had even begun to run the water or strip off her clothes there came a knock on the door. She recognised it immediately, four raps with a pause after the first two. Jarrett Brent! Lord, what was he doing back again? What did he want now?

She ran down the stairs and yanked open the door. 'What are you doing here?' she asked ungraciously.

'We had a date; have you forgotten?' His blue eyes looked her over, observing the smudges of dirt, her creased clothes. His mouth twisted wryly. 'I guess you did.'

'Our date isn't until half-past seven,' she pointed out coldly, her eyes flashing her fury.

He made a great show of looking at his watch, and then he showed it to Saira, and she nearly died. 'It's not that time already? Heavens, I didn't know. I'm sorry, you'd better come in and wait; I was just going to have a bath.'

His brows rose curiously. 'A bath? How have you managed to get hot water?'

'I haven't.'

'Then you're either very stupid or very brave.' He followed her into the sitting-room.

'I have no choice.'

'Oh, but you do; you can come up to the Hall. Get whatever you need; my car's outside.' His voice brooked no argument.

Their eyes did battle but in the end Saira gave in. The thought of really hot water and sweetly scented soap was too much. She would wash her hair as well; it took ages to dry but he would have to wait, this was too good an opportunity to miss.

In two minutes flat Saira was ready, a clean dress, undies, shoes, her hairdryer, all in a supermarket plastic bag.

Jarrett eyed it with amusement. 'Very chic.'

'I only have a suitcase besides my handbag,' she snapped. 'I suppose you're thinking that your girlfriend wouldn't be seen dead carrying her possessions in something like this, unless it happened to be one of Harrods'. But as far as I'm concerned it's functional and you can laugh all you like.'

'I'm not laughing,' he assured her.

'But you're mocking, and that's just as bad.' She slammed the door behind them and put the key safely into her handbag.

His car was a white Mercedes with cream leather seats, luxurious in the extreme. Saira hoped she did not mark it. She had not realised her aunt's cottage was so dusty. So far she had only whisked over the rooms she was using, waiting to see the outcome of her legal battle before giving it a thorough clean.

There was no point in wasting her energy if the cottage ended up belonging to Jarrett Brent, not when he was going to do some alterations. The thought grated. It would be such a pity. It had been like this for so many years; why change it? It wasn't as if it lacked in anything—it had a bathroom and a halfway decent kitchen, and there were fireplaces in all the rooms. It was such a cosy cottage.

She was thankful the journey to Frenton Hall was only short. The impact of Jarrett Brent sitting beside her was too powerful for words; she had never expected anything like this when she slid into the seat. The essence of him filled the car and she found the atmosphere stifling. She wanted to wind down her window and take deep breaths of fresh air, but knew that to do so would invite comment, and so she sat there, her hands folded neatly in her lap, concentrating on her breathing.

Saira felt rather than saw Jarrett look at her, and on each occasion a tingle ran down her spine and she thought of her dream and the closeness of their bodies and she wanted to edge away. It was madness, she knew, and yet there was nothing she could do about it. The feelings were there, unwanted, roller-coasting through her veins, setting every nerve-end on edge. She was grateful when they arrived.

Mrs Gibbs was nowhere in sight as he opened the oak door. 'It's my housekeeper's night off,' he explained, as though he knew exactly what she was thinking, and Saira felt a further moment's unease; she had counted on the woman as a chaperon. But she did not let her fear show, following him indoors and heading immediately for the stairs.

'Will you show me where the bathroom is?'

The wide, shallow staircase was carpeted in red, and each of the three tiers was held up with an Ionic column with a scroll-like ornamentation at the top. It was very impressive and Saira had never felt so out of place in her life.

He took her along a corridor lined with portraits—she guessed they were his ancestors though there was no time to study them now—and finally opened a door at the end. 'Here we are, you can use this one. I think you'll find everything you need. Just yell out if you don't.'

And have him come running? Not likely. 'I'm sure I'll be all right,' she said quietly, moving inside and immediately bolting the door. At last she felt safe.

She stood for a moment looking round her at the white marble and gold tiled floor, at the solid gold taps and fittings—or at the very least gold-plated! A monstrous bathtub in deep ruby, a shower cubicle, matching ruby towels, soaps and lotions, even new toothbrushes—everything anyone could wish for.

The choice now was a shower or a bath? A shower would be quicker but the thought of luxuriating in hot scented water was too much. In minutes the bath was filled and Saira slid slowly into its perfumed, bubbly depths. Never had a tub of hot water felt so good. It was heaven, sheer heaven. She took the band off her plait and undid her hair, letting it float out around her. Time lost all meaning.

It was not until she heard a sharp rap on the door and Jarrett enquiring whether she was all right that Saira came to with a start. 'I won't be long,' she promised, glad she had slid the bolt, because she wouldn't have put it past him to walk in.

She quickly finished washing herself and then shampooed her hair in the sink, towelling it roughly dry before pampering her body with an exotic lotion she found on a shelf. She pulled on her pink cotton dress, slipped her feet into her sandals, and went back out into the corridor. She needed somewhere now to dry her hair. Perhaps one of the bedrooms?

The first door revealed a room that was as opulent as the bathroom, convincing her that all the rooms were the same. She had already seen the library and the breakfast-room and the magnificent hall. It was an incredible house.

She plugged in her hairdrier and sat on a stool in front of the dressing table, bending her head forward, lifting her hair frequently with her fingers so that the diffused heat could get to it.

She did not see or hear Jarrett enter, knew only of his presence when his hand touched her shoulder. She jumped as though she were bitten. 'Goodness, you frightened me.'

'I've been calling you. It's no wonder you didn't hear. Please, allow me.' Without waiting for an answer he took the drier, holding it to her hair, lifting its heavy length as he had seen her do—but there was a difference!

His touch was a caress, intentionally sensual, evoking sensations that amazed her. They were so like her dream—and her immediate and unwanted and unreasonable response to his kiss—that it frightened her. She knew why he was doing it. He wanted her on his side; he didn't want to fight her, he wanted her to happily accept that the cottage was his.

CHAPTER FOUR

JARRETT BRENT was a devious swine and Saira hated him, but rather than cause a scene she sat very still and let him get on with drying her hair. She would pretend indifference, not let him see the electric effect he was having on her, and hope he would not hear the wild thump of her heart. How she could feel like this and hate him at the same time she did not know. It was weird.

'You have beautiful hair,' he murmured as he concentrated totally on his self-imposed task. 'Why do you always wear it in a pigtail?'

Plaited, it reached her waist, but with it hanging loose Saira could sit on it. There had been a time when she'd considered having it cut, but her father had always adored her hair and for his sake, for his memory, she had refrained. 'Because it's easier,' she told him, 'because it gets in the way if I leave it loose, because it knots up too quickly.'

'But it's criminal to hide such beautiful hair,' he protested. 'You should flaunt it, Saira. It's enough to drive a man insane.' He said her name so easily that it made her wonder how often he thought of her this way, whether the Miss Carlton was for effect.

He buried his face in it, sniffing appreciatively, and Saira watched him through the mirror. His expression was different from any she had yet seen, softer than usual, all the harshness gone, his eyes half hidden by lowered lids, fully intent on what he was doing.

Suddenly he looked up and caught her watching him and for a brief instant she saw the naked desire, masked instantly by a smile. 'I could get carried away. I've never met a woman with hair like yours before.'

Saira's heart beat rapidly and uneasily. She had to be careful what she said or did; she was at this man's mercy, in an extremely vulnerable position. Things could get out of hand if she did not watch them. 'I think it's dry enough,' she said, and was surprised by how husky her voice sounded.

Jarrett immediately switched off the drier and unplugged it, and when he said, 'Where is your brush?' Saira passionately wished she had taken advantage of those few seconds to get up.

'You're not doing it,' she protested quickly; she simply could not stand his nearness any longer. It was suffocating; it was doing her no good at all.

Their eyes met again in the mirror, his blue and very intent, his hands resting gently and almost possessively on her shoulders. 'Oh, but I am,' he insisted. 'And surely it's a very little thing to let me do?' His voice was so low it was almost a growl.

But an intimate job, she thought unhappily; this was not the sort of relationship she wanted with him. She wanted to keep her distance, she wanted to maintain a barrier between them. 'I prefer to brush my own hair, thank you,' she said primly. 'You've done enough for me.'

'Have you ever had a man brush it for you?' he asked. Still his eyes were watchful; insistent, persuasive, sensual!

Saira shook her head. Tony had never even suggested it. He had liked her hair but it wasn't a big thing with him. This man was making it seem as though it had the power to turn him on. Perhaps he had a fetish about hair? Perhaps he couldn't resist it? Perhaps this was the only reason he was interested in her?

'It's one of a woman's biggest assets,' Jarrett went on, and without more ado he plucked her brush from the top of her bag and began stroking it through the full length of her hair; long, sensual strokes, each one slow and full of meaning.

Saira kept her eyes closed, she could not, would not, look at him. She had no wish to see the pleasure on his face; it was positively indecent—and definitely, most definitely exciting!

'You're taking an unfair advantage,' she said in protest, though her voice lacked conviction. 'I knew it was wrong to come here; I should never have let you pressure me.'

'But surely your bath was much pleasanter than a cold dip? And this certainly is for me.' As if to add emphasis to his words he not only stroked her hair but felt the shape of her head as well, his fingers long and strong, gentle, seeking, inciting.

Saira felt pleasures of the sort experienced in her dream. 'But it isn't what I expected,' she complained sharply, 'and I don't want you to do it. It's wrong, all wrong, you're a stranger, you shouldn't be doing this, I shouldn't be letting you.'

'Will you wear it loose for the rest of the night?' It was as though he hadn't listened to one word she'd said, as though he had a one-track mind and refused to deviate.

Saira looked at his reflection coldly. 'I don't think so. It's so fine it's not practical. The slightest breeze and it flies everywhere.'

'Isn't that part of the beauty?' There was a sort of reverence on his face as he performed the task, an enjoyment that was unreal. This certainly wasn't the man who had been baiting her about the cottage.

She closed her eyes again, unable to handle the situation. 'What are you trying to do to me?' she asked, unaware of the huskiness in her tone. 'And what would Joy say if she saw you now?'

He smiled. 'There's nothing serious between Joy and myself, we have a very open relationship.'

Saira looked at him in total disbelief. 'You mean that you're each free to go out with someone else?' It certainly wasn't what it had looked like to her. The girl doted on him. He had to be lying.

'Something like that,' he agreed, and his smile was such that Saira did not know whether to believe him or not.

'Where does she live?' At least it was better to be talking about someone else.

'In Coxwold.'

A neighbouring village, realised Saira. 'Do you see much of her?'

'Quite a lot, yes, but why are we talking about Joy when you're here? It's you I want to talk about; it's you I'm interested in right at this very moment.'

'Then you shouldn't be,' she snapped. 'You shouldn't be doing this; I shouldn't have let you. I've told you before I don't want any sort of relationship—regardless what your arrangement with Joy is.' She rose to her feet and took the brush off him. 'Thank you, that's enough.'

'A pity. I could go on all night.' His smile was cool and calm, his whole demeanour unruffled.

His total command of the situation was in complete contrast to her uncharacteristic hot-headedness, thought Saira, and it infuriated her all the more. Why couldn't she remain cool too? She wasn't usually this impetuous;

what was wrong with her? She began to plait her hair
with quick, hasty movements until Jarrett put out a hand
to stop her.

'Please, don't do that.'

And like a fool she gave in. But she vowed to herself
that this would be the only time. In future she would—
Saira stopped herself. What was she thinking about,
future? There was no future where this man was concerned. There was here and now, a matter of possession
to be cleared up, and then the end. There would be no
more baths here at Frenton Hall, no more hair-brushing
sessions, no more intimacies of any kind. Jarrett Brent
would be out of sight and out of mind.

When she left the room and made her way back
downstairs Saira was conscious of Jarrett close behind;
she could feel his eyes on her, was aware of his raw masculinity, and it was all she could do to stop herself turning
around and screaming at him to leave her alone. She did
not want any of this, she couldn't handle it.

She was shocked to see by the grandfather clock in
the hall that it was a quarter to nine. She looked at Jarrett
with wide eyes. 'I had no idea I'd been so long. It's too
late to go out now, of course; I'd better get back to the
cottage and——'

'Oh, no,' he growled, 'you're not getting away that
easily. We can still get a meal, or we can even eat here.
The choice is yours. But whatever you do, don't think
this is the end of the evening.' He leaned insouciantly
against one of the Doric columns as he waited for her
answer, casual, relaxed, knowing that without a doubt
he was going to get his own way.

Saira groaned inwardly. 'OK, we'll eat out,' she said.
Remaining in this house with Jarrett Brent for a further
two or three hours would be intolerable and totally dis-

astrous. She had a very strong idea how it might end—
and she wanted to avoid that at all costs. He had such
an overpowering presence, such a strong sexual personality, that it would be difficult, if not impossible, to resist
him should he press his advantage. The dream had been
enough to contend with. How could she cope in real life?

He took her to the Fauconberg Arms in Coxwold and
she tried not to think that it was here where Joy lived,
that they had probably eaten here many times, and
maybe even the staff would think it strange that Jarrett
was here with a different girl. Or did he bring many girls
here? Was that what he meant by his open relationship?
She was not at all sure that she believed him when he
said there was nothing serious between them, and if he
was lying he was hardly being fair on the girl.

They parked on the cobbled frontage of the seven-
teenth-century inn and inside the atmosphere was
pleasant and cosy. They ordered drinks and studied the
menu and Saira felt strange sitting with The Enemy, as
she had dubbed him. She tried hard to push away her
awareness of this big man, not to feel the warmth of his
body, or smell the pungency of his aftershave, but it was
difficult. The dream was still so vivid, his kiss so clear,
her body so aroused; she wondered when the feelings
would go away.

Jarrett surprisingly ordered champagne to go with their
meal and Saira looked at him in amazement. 'What are
we celebrating?' As far as she was concerned, champagne was only drunk on special occasions like wed-
dings and anniversaries and special birthdays, and this
certainly wasn't special in any sort of way.

Jarrett spread his hands expressively, a twinkle in his
eyes. 'I thought it would be rather nice. Does there have
to be a reason?'

'I think so.' She deliberately kept her tone cool and impersonal.

'Then—we'll think of one. The beginning of a new friendship, perhaps?' The inevitable smile was in place, annoying her intensely.

She said nothing but looked doubtful.

Brows rose. 'You don't agree?'

'How can I be friends with a man who is trying to take my cottage from me?' she asked sharply. Lord, he was so insensitive it was unbelievable.

Jarrett put his hand on hers across the table, warm and gentle, persuasive, designed to placate her. 'No, Saira, you have it all wrong. I am not trying to take anything from you.'

'Then what are you trying to do?' she demanded, snatching away. She did not want him to touch her; she wanted to rid herself of these feelings, not enhance them. It was actually better when they argued, because then she could forget he was a raw, sensual male who sent her body into confusion, and her mind into terror.

'I am trying to set matters straight,' he said. 'How can I take something from you that is not yours?'

The gall of the man! 'But it is mine,' she insisted, 'and if you don't believe me now, time will tell. The truth will come out eventually, you can be very sure of that.' She met the blueness of his eyes with a challenge in hers.

'I imagine it will,' he said, much to her surprise. 'The truth always does.' But the easiness with which he agreed did nothing to assuage Saira's anger; he was humouring her and she didn't like it. It was going to be a long-drawn-out battle for sure.

And then, with a sudden, surprising change of subject, he said, 'Tell me about yourself.'

Saira lifted her shoulders. 'There's nothing of any real interest to relate. I'm the youngest of three sisters, I live with my mother, my father died when I was sixteen, and that's about it.'

'What do you do for a living?'

He sounded genuinely interested, though Saira could not be sure. It was probably all part and parcel of his devious plot. 'I'm a pharmacist.'

His brows lifted. 'Now that is interesting; I've never met a pharmacist before. Did you have to do much training?'

She nodded. 'Three years at university to get my degree and then a further one year's hands-on experience at our local hospital.'

He pulled down the corners of his mouth expressively. 'I'm impressed. I didn't realise you had to work so hard. If I'd had to guess what you did for a living I'd probably have said you were a teacher. What made you decide to become a pharmacist?'

Saira shrugged. 'I guess I've always been curious as to how medicines were made. I can remember mixing up various potions for my dolls when I was little. At one time I wanted to be a scientist, I wanted to discover new medicines, but then I changed my mind and decided to be a pharmacist instead.'

'And do you like your work?'

'Very much.' Talking about something other than the cottage, Saira was able to relax. 'I find it quite challenging. A pharmacist does a lot more than just dispense medicines, as some people think. We're highly qualified and in many cases can save people a visit to their doctor.'

'I'll remember that next time I'm feeling ill,' he said with his usual sardonic grin. 'I think I might quite like your cool hands on my brow.'

Feeling sure he was goading her, Saira declined to answer and he changed the subject yet again and asked her what kind of music she liked.

'What's the point in all of this?' Saira asked, forgetting that she had once been guilty of questioning him. 'Once we've sorted out our dispute over Honeysuckle Cottage we won't be seeing each other again.'

'That would be a pity.' His voice was suddenly low and urgent, his eyes narrowed and masked so that it was difficult to read his expression. 'I would like to see more of you, Saira.'

Her own eyes flashed a brilliant green. 'The feeling's not mutual, I assure you.' But her heartbeats quickened at the thought. Even though this man was totally abhorrent to her, she could not quell the sensations he managed to arouse. It was insanity and yet there was nothing she could do about it. She could only be thankful that he could not see what was going on inside her.

'What is it that you've got against me?' he rasped, his tone hard all of a sudden, his blue eyes cool now, his mouth without its usual curve. He was evidently not used to being turned down.

'Absolutely everything,' she cried, and then, realising that she had raised her voice and people were looking, she went on more quietly, 'Surely you know? It's got to be obvious what I think about you.'

'You think I'm trying to trick you out of your aunt's cottage?' There was a sudden, thoughtful expression on his face.

'Yes, I do, as a matter of fact,' she retorted. 'I don't think anything is as straight-cut as you're making out. I think you're a liar and a——'

He cut in abruptly. 'Would it help matters if I made a present of it to you?'

Saira gasped. 'A present, of my own property? You're crazy. You'd please me more by confessing the truth.' And because she had had enough of this conversation, because she knew it was getting her nowhere, because it was getting completely out of hand, she pointed and said, 'Oh, look, a mouse.'

Jarrett touched the table leg in front of him, running his finger over the smooth rodent which was carved into the oak. 'You've surely heard of Robert Thompson of Kilburn?'

Saira frowned and shook her head. Kilburn was a neighbouring village, she knew, but she had never heard of Robert Thompson.

'The famous wood carver?'

'No, I don't think so.' She took a sip of her Campari.

'I thought Elizabeth would have told you about him. The mouse was his trademark. He used to carve one into every piece of furniture he made—the tradition is still carried on.'

'But why a mouse?' she asked. It was good to be talking civilly for once.

'Originally he was a wheelwright,' Jarrett told her, 'but he made some bits and pieces for the local church and the priest was so impressed that he told him he ought to specialise in oak furniture—and so he did. And when he was trying to think of a symbol to characterise his work he thought of the expression, "poor as a church mouse". The mouse became an integral part of everything he made and he very soon became world-famous.'

'How interesting,' exclaimed Saira. 'I really never knew that.'

'But we've got off the subject, we were talking about Honeysuckle Cottage.'

'Oh, yes,' she replied, groaning inwardly that he had not been completely side-tracked, 'you were trying to be magnaminous. I'm afraid talk like that doesn't wash with me, Mr Brent. The cottage is mine, there's no doubt about it. You'll be getting a letter from Mr Kirby tomorrow.' She hadn't meant to say that, she had wanted it to come as a complete surprise. But as usual her tongue had run away with her and now she looked at him closely, watching for his reaction.

'Really?'

She was disappointed at the indifferent answer. 'Yes, really,' she hissed. 'So this time you'll have to tell the truth.'

'You mean I'll have to dig up the deeds?' he asked with a wicked smile.

'*If* you have them,' she cried. What she wouldn't give to knock that smile off his face. God, he was infuriating. 'What did Mr Kirby have to say?'

'That my aunt never mentioned selling her property,' she retorted.

'In other words, he's calling me a liar as well?' But he did not look upset by the thought.

'Not exactly,' said Saira, her chin high. 'We just want the truth.'

Their conversation came to an abrupt end when they were told that their table was ready and Saira was not sorry. There was so little she could say that made any difference. Jarrett always made sure that he came out on top.

In the small restaurant they were seated in front of the window. It was a long, narrow room with pink table-cloths and candles, and from here Saira could see down its entire length. She was glad they were not tucked into a corner; the thought of being secluded with Jarrett Brent did not appeal in the least.

For her first course Saira had prawn cocktail, Jarrett lentil soup, and they ate in silence. The champagne he had ordered sat in its bucket of crushed ice at the side of their table and Saira hoped he was not expecting her to drink very much.

It was a pleasant, oak-beamed room with old prints on the walls and subdued lighting, and under other circumstances she might have enjoyed it, but tonight Saira was seething. She felt sure that Jarrett Brent had some ulterior motive for inviting her out, she could not accept that he had done it out of the kindness of his heart. It was all to do with Honeysuckle Cottage. The conversation was by no means at an end.

Their champagne was poured by a smiling waitress and their empty dishes taken away. Jarrett raised his glass. 'Here's to friendship.'

'I can't drink to that,' Saira said firmly. 'I have no wish to become your friend.' She lifted her glass. 'How about good health?' It was a nice, neutral sort of toast.

'Good health—*and* friendship,' he insisted.

Saira said nothing, let him think he had won. The bubbles tickled her nose and she put her glass down after one tiny sip. Champagne always went to her head and it was imperative that she keep a clear mind. It would be so easy, so very easy for this man to seduce her. She still found it incredibly difficult to understand how her body could act this way when she hated him so much.

She looked through the window at the street outside, she looked down the length of the room at the other diners, she looked anywhere but at Jarrett Brent.

'Am I completely abhorrent to you, Saira?' he asked tersely.

She had not realised he was watching her. 'Not exactly,' she confessed, finally looking at him, wishing their main course would arrive so that she would have something on which to concentrate.

'Then why are you behaving as though I'm not here?' His deep blue eyes were narrowed and cold, sending a chill through her veins, making her shiver. A muscle jerked in his jaw and his usually generous lips were compressed into a tight line.

'Am I?' she asked with professed innocence.

'Dammit, you know you are,' he muttered.

'And you're not used to being ignored by your companion, is that what you're saying? It's bad for your ego? Joy, and all your other lady friends, enjoy your company, are only too willing to go out with you, to give you their undivided attention. It must be quite a change to meet someone like me.'

'It's exceptional,' he agreed curtly.

Her eyes flashed. 'It's your own fault if you're not enjoying yourself; you can't blame me. I didn't want to come.' She scooped up her glass and took a long, savage swallow of champagne.

Their main course arrived and she was quiet until the waitress had gone then she said tersely, 'I would prefer to change the subject. I'm fed up with talking about me and the cottage. Let's turn the tables: tell me about yourself instead.'

Saira had ordered a simple lasagne verdi, and was surprised when it arrived with an excellent side-salad of exotic fruits, endive, radicchio and red and white cabbage, as well as the more normal lettuce, tomato and cucumber. It was all very tastefully arranged in a spiral on her plate. She picked up a piece of kiwi fruit on the end of her fork and looked at him as she put it between her teeth.

He frowned. 'I would, if I thought you were really interested.'

'I am.'

'So much so that you're here under duress?' he accused. 'So much so that you think of me as your enemy?' There was a harshness to his tone and anger in his eyes.

Saira shrugged. 'Then don't tell me if you don't want to. I thought it would pass the evening.'

'Are you finding it incredibly boring already?'

'Let's say I've had better times,' she said primly, taking a timid forkful of the piping hot lasagne. It was delicious.

He swung his head in an angry gesture and jabbed his knife into his steak and at that moment they were approached by no other than Joy Woodstock.

'Jarrett!' the pretty girl exclaimed. 'I was walking past and thought it was you; I simply had to come in and make sure.' She did not even glance at Saira; all her attention devoted on the handsome man.

He immediately sprang to his feet. 'Joy, what a delightful surprise. Will you join us?'

'Goodness, no,' the girl exclaimed. 'I've already eaten, and it's unlike you to be here so late.' Finally she looked at Saira but there was no smile on her face, in fact she looked positively hostile, making it perfectly clear she was unhappy about the situation.

If Saira hadn't been suspicious before about Jarrett's statement that he and Joy had an open relationship she was now. The girl was livid, and surely she wouldn't be like that if they weren't serious about each other? He had probably made the whole thing up to suit himself; he was probably as bad as Tony, flirting with other girls behind Joy's back. She suddenly felt sorry for her.

Saira waited for Jarrett's explanation, but there was none forthcoming. He merely said, 'That's a shame. Saira and I would have loved your company, isn't that so, Saira?'

'He took pity on me,' she said instead. 'I do apologise if I've taken over your boyfriend for the evening.'

Jarrett frowned at this unexpected comment. Joy looked surprised, but then she smiled and gazed at Jarrett adoringly. 'He's so kind, he has a heart of gold.' She leaned down and kissed him full on the lips. 'I'll see you tomorrow, darling.' And she smiled again at Saira, though behind the smile there was a warning. Hands off, it said, this is my man. And as far as Saira was concerned she was welcome to him.

When she had gone Saira said, 'Joy wasn't at all happy to see me here with you. I think you were lying when you said there was nothing serious between you.'

He shook his head. 'Not at all, she was just surprised.'

'Surprised?' echoed Saira. 'Shocked and angry, I would say. Do you know what I think? I think you're the same as all men; I don't think you know what it means to be true to one girl.'

Brows rose and he seemed startled by her sudden, verbal attack. 'That's your considered opinion of the male race in general, is it?'

Saira nodded.

'And how have you reached that conclusion?'

'By experience,' she snapped, feeling sure he wasn't really all that interested.

Thick brows rose. 'Tell me about it.'

'Why should I?' she demanded. 'Suffice it to say that I've been well and truly let down.'

'What was his name?'

She frowned. 'What has that got to do with it?'

Jarrett shrugged. 'It sometimes helps to talk. Was it recent? Is that why you're so prickly?'

'As a matter of fact, it was,' she told him, 'but it has nothing to do with the way I feel about you.' Which was a lie, because she had already placed him in the same category.

'It's just the cottage that bothers you?'

'Yes.'

'Not my kisses? Not when I brush your hair? Not when I say you're beautiful?' He watched her closely as he spoke, his eyes registering every nuance on her face, seeing the faint flush, the uncertainty, the doubt.

'Most definitely not,' she lied again. 'If you want the truth, I can't stand you.'

He laughed, a loud guffaw that had other diners looking at them. 'But you're drawn to me against your will? That's the top and bottom of it, isn't it?'

Saira did not know how he could possibly have guessed but she was going to deny it to the hilt. 'You're crazy. You're the last man I'd feel attracted to.'

His lips quirked and his eyes glinted. 'Something tells me you're lying.'

'Why would I lie?' she snapped. 'Lord, how could I possibly be attracted to you when all you're intent on is doing me out of my inheritance?'

'Circumstances have nothing to do with attraction; it hits when you're least expecting it.' His blue eyes were, as always, penetratingly sharp.

'Maybe,' she admitted, 'but not in this case, not with you. It's the joke of the century. Once this matter's sorted out I never want to see you again.' And she had no doubt in her mind about that.

'Which obviously means you're accepting that Honeysuckle Cottage is mine?' There was a pleased smile on his face as he spoke.

'No it does not,' replied Saira sharply.

'But *if* you were proved right—and I don't mind telling you it's a very big if—but if you were proved right and you came to live here, then we would, without a doubt, see something of each other.' His cool smile was exceedingly confident.

'Not if I could help it,' she insisted, while at the same time the very thought caused her heart to quicken its beats. They would be neighbours, they would undoubtedly bump into one another, although with them both working it would not be very frequent. She rarely saw her own neighbours at home and they lived right next door—so it was nothing to worry about.

They had almost finished their meal when Jarrett said, 'I've enjoyed tonight, very much. We must do it again. How about tomorrow?'

Saira looked at him with wide, shocked eyes. 'With a bit of luck, if you respond to Mr Kirby's letter, I won't be here by tomorrow. But in any case I thought you were seeing Joy?'

He shrugged. 'Only in passing, so to speak. She works for me.'

'Oh!' Saira's fine brows rose. 'Doing what?' This was something she had definitely not expected.

Her astonishment amused him; he smiled widely. 'She looks after my horses.'

'Your horses?' she queried, shocked even further.

'Don't look so surprised,' he said with a laugh. 'Joy's marvellous with them.'

Saira shook her head. 'She looks too delicate. How many horses do you have?' This man was full of surprises.

'Just two.'

'And you have to employ someone to look after them?' she asked sceptically. It didn't make sense. He had obviously created the job so that Joy would be there whenever he felt like amusing himself.

'Sometimes my work takes me away from home and they need their exercise,' he explained. 'She not only exercises them, she cleans the stables, grooms them, does everything. She's invaluable to me.'

'Then why do you keep them if you don't have time to look after them?' Saira asked.

'Because I love horses, and when I do have the time it's the perfect relaxation.'

'So what are you too busy doing?' She wondered if he would answer her question this time.

'I'm a land and property developer,' he announced, and then, as if she could not possibly find it of any interest, 'Do you ride, Saira?'

She lifted her shoulders. 'Not very well. I used to ride a friend's horse, many, many years ago, but I'm no expert.'

He smiled suddenly. 'Then tomorrow you must come and see my horses, and we'll go out riding together.'

CHAPTER FIVE

'WHERE are you going?' Saira questioned when Jarrett Brent drove straight past Honeysuckle Cottage. They had finished their meal in virtual silence; half of the bottle of Roederer Cristal was left—such a waste of money, she thought. She could have fed herself and her mother for two weeks on what that bottle must have cost.

'I thought we'd go back to the Hall for a nightcap.' Jarrett glanced across at her as he spoke and there was challenge in his eyes, as though he knew she was likely to object.

And object she did. 'Not on your life, it's a rotten idea, I refuse to come. Drop me off right here.' She had her hand on the handle ready to jump out.

'But you left your bag and your dirty clothes,' he pointed out. 'You can at least come and pick them up.' He made no attempt to slow down.

'They're not important,' Saira said firmly. 'I demand you stop this car right now.'

She might have been speaking to a brick wall; he carried on at speed and when she looked across at him he was smiling, a smile that suggested he was going to get his own way no matter what. 'Do you always go against a girl's wishes?' she asked angrily.

'Only when I think it's a token protest,' he assured her, still smiling, still looking supremely confident.

'This is no token protest,' she asserted fiercely, 'I mean it.'

But it made no difference, he still did not stop until they reached his home. He did not use the main entrance, driving instead along a private lane to the back of the Hall, another pair of heavy iron gates opening by remote control—which was a pity, she thought, because she could have jumped out and run while he was opening them. No doubt he had guessed this was in her mind and that was the reason he had come this way. He seemed to know her every thought.

'Here we are,' he said, and as they entered the huge building, his hand on her elbow as he guided her, Saira was conscious of the fact that they were alone, completely alone, and that she was very, very vulnerable. Even more so than at the beginning of the evening.

All the hours spent together had had a very profound effect on her; her heartbeats quickened and she decided there and then that she would get away as quickly as she could. One drink and she would leave.

He took her through to a cosy sitting-room, switching on lights along the corridors as they walked. Saira remained silent, not looking forward one little bit to spending more time with Jarrett, especially here where she felt she was at his mercy. She wondered how many times he had entertained Joy in this house, how many nightcaps they had had, how often the girl had spent the night. Was that what he was expecting her to do?

'Now,' he said, when he had settled her in the blue and beige room which was more homely than some of the others, less elegant, more relaxing. 'What would you like? Martini? Gin? Vodka? Whisky? Another Campari? Or a liqueur perhaps? Brandy? Tia Maria? Cointreau? Crème de menthe?'

Saira shook her head to all of these. 'I'll have hot chocolate, please.'

The expression on his face was comical. 'Chocolate?' he queried, as if it were an unheard of word. 'Are you serious?'

'Yes, of course I am.' She found it difficult to keep her face straight.

'I doubt we have any.'

'Then I'll have coffee,' she said with a shrug. 'Decaffeinated. I'll make it myself if it's any trouble.'

'It's not exactly the type of nightcap I had in mind.' He stood frowning down at her in the deep, comfortable armchair.

'I know it isn't,' she said, 'but it's what I want. I've already had sufficient to drink.' More than enough in fact. Her head was quite light from two glasses of champagne and her earlier Campari. 'What did you think, that I'd be a pushover? That you could bring me back here, get me drunk, and then take me to bed? Was that what you had in mind?' Her tone was heated.

A vicious frown slammed across his brow. 'Have I ever given you reason to doubt my integrity?'

There was the kiss in the kitchen earlier today—dared she recall that? But otherwise he had done nothing out of order; he had brushed her hair, but the feelings he evoked were all in her mind; he hadn't done anything wrong. She shook her head. 'I suppose not.'

'Then you're mighty suspicious for no reason. Or did your ex-boyfriend behave that way? Perhaps you tar us all with the same brush because of him? Did he force you into bed against your will once he'd had a drink, once he'd got you drunk? Did the whole situation become intolerable? Is that what's wrong with you? Are you afraid of men now?'

'Tony was a gentleman,' she snapped. Tony had never drunk; he was an absolute teetotaller. His father had died of alcoholism and it had put Tony off drinking for ever, and she rarely had anything herself; that was why she had to be so careful now. Even a moderate amount of alcohol went very quickly to her head; she had already gone well over her quota.

'If he was so perfect, why did you finish with him?' sneered Jarrett.

'Because, if you must know,' Saira retorted, unable to keep the words back now, 'he was seeing someone else behind my back; he was double-crossing me, and if I were Joy I'd give you your marching orders as well.'

'Joy and I have a perfect understanding,' he said, and although he smiled it was insincere, leaving Saira completely unsure as to what their exact relationship was. 'I'll go and make the coffee,' he added.

Saira had half a mind to creep out and run home while he was busying himself in the kitchen, but for some reason she did not understand she stayed, and when he returned she was almost asleep in the chair.

She heard him come in but it was with difficulty that she lifted her eyelids. She saw him through her lashes and with the outline of him softened he looked more human and she smiled. 'I almost dropped off.'

'It is late and you've had a long day,' he agreed. He set their two cups down on a low table and took a chair at right angles to her.

Saira felt warm and comfortable and wanted to shut her eyes again, wanted to shut this man out and go to sleep. But she knew it would be impossible. His presence would be far too tangible; she was aware of him like no other man, seemed to breathe him into her pores, something she had never done where Tony was concerned.

It was strange, this feeling. Jarrett Brent was her number one enemy, he professed to own her cottage, her inheritance; she hated him with every breath in her body, and yet . . .

'What was that sigh for?'

Saira had not even realised that she'd sighed, nor that he was watching her, and she had no intention now of disclosing her thoughts. 'I'm tired, that's all. I want to go home.'

'You could always sleep here.'

'And that's the real reason you've brought me back, isn't it?' she questioned sharply.

His eyes narrowed angrily. 'You're doing me an injustice, Saira. I can assure you I have no ulterior motive, I'm thinking of your comfort, that's all. Why don't you trust me?'

It was a simple question, yet difficult to answer. Why didn't she trust him? Or was it herself she didn't trust? Was she beginning to feel something for Jarrett Brent?

'Is it too difficult a question?' His lips were grim, his deep blue eyes watchful.

'I don't trust you because you've taken my cottage,' she said finally.

Jarrett shook his head. 'That isn't what we're talking about.'

'It amounts to the same thing.'

'Does it?' he asked. 'I don't think so, Saira. I think what you're afraid of is *your* feelings. I think that's the real problem.'

'What do you mean?' she asked sharply. He had hit the nail so accurately on the head that she wanted to cringe, wanted to sink back into the chair and disappear. He had no right guessing her innermost thoughts.

'I think that deep down inside you don't find me as abhorrent as you make out,' he said evenly, 'but you feel that you must fight me because of the cottage, and you're fighting your own feelings into the bargain. It's yourself you don't trust.'

'Nonsense!' she flung back. 'The only reason I'm fighting *is* because of Honeysuckle Cottage. It means a lot to me.'

He looked at her for a long, calculating moment. 'Exactly what does it represent? Security? Nostalgia? Or is it money in the bank if you were to sell? Is that what's bothering you? You were hoping to make yourself a pretty penny out of it?'

Saira snorted indelicately, angrily. 'I would never sell, I love that cottage—and my aunt wanted me to have it. I shall fight it out to the bitter end. Where are those deeds?'

His lips quirked. 'In my estate manager's filing system.'

'I think you're lying.'

'You can think what you like.'

'It's ridiculous to say that you can't find them in his absence,' she said sharply. 'What's wrong with telephoning him?'

'I didn't realise the matter was so urgent.' And still he was laughing at her, mocking, casual, cool, fully in control of the situation.

Saira grew even more uptight. 'It's not urgent in that sense of the word, but you know very well that I want this matter sorted out before I return home. I can't take time off indefinitely.'

'And what will you do when I produce the deeds?' Still he was smiling in that infuriating way that made her want to strike out at him.

'Have them verified, of course,' she snapped.

'You wouldn't go straight back home?'

'Not until I was sure the cottage was legally yours.'

'And after that I wouldn't see you again?'

Her fine brows rose. 'As far as I'm concerned that would be a good thing. You're bad news; you're the worst thing that's ever happened to me.'

His lips tightened at her sharp words. 'I've been called many things in my time, Saira, but never bad news. Drink your coffee before it gets cold.'

She did as he asked and then stood up. 'It's time I went,' she said abruptly.

'You don't have to,' he said, rising too.

'I'll give you ten out of ten for persistence,' she flashed, 'but I intend to go.'

'It can't be pleasant in that cottage on your own.'

She eyed him scornfully. 'As if *you* care! But it doesn't worry me; I'll stay until I've proved that it's mine.'

He inclined his head. 'I have to admit that you've impressed me. I didn't think you'd stick it out for as long as you have.'

'That's because you don't know me,' she snapped. 'I have a very stubborn nature, Mr Brent.'

He frowned at her formality but when she made to move his hands came down on her shoulders, halting her, steadying her, surprisingly gentle and yet holding her prisoner at the same time.

Her eyes shot wide and she looked into his face. 'What the hell do you think you're doing?' She deliberately made her voice cold.

'You're very beautiful, Saira, the most stubborn, beautiful girl I've ever met. You drive a man crazy, do you know that?'

Saira eyed him coldly, hiding the stampede of her pulses. No girl could be immune to such flattery. But fight it she must. 'So I was right, this is why you invited me back,' she snapped. 'Let us get one thing clear, I don't want to be kissed by you, or touched by you, or anything else by you. All I want is the cottage.' Her voice rose with each set of words until in the end she was almost shouting.

He drew in a swift, angry breath but he didn't let her go; instead the pressure of his fingers increased. 'Saira, why keep fighting? We both know that deep down inside you're attracted to me. Why don't——?'

Saira cut in sharply. 'That's a mighty big ego you've got, *Mr* Brent. I am *not* attracted to you, I never will be; all I want is to settle the matter of Honeysuckle Cottage.'

When he gripped her shoulders even more tightly Saira thought for a moment that he was going to shake her, to vent his fury, but he remained still and silent. His eyes looked into hers, a deep, intent, hypnotic blue that held her locked in a gaze she wanted to break away from—but somehow couldn't.

She felt an unexpected, unwanted warmth creep through her body and knew that if she didn't get away she would give in to the insane feelings that were growing inside her. It was a sensation she had never experienced—except in her dream—and it was one she desperately wanted to dissociate herself from, but couldn't.

In the beginning she had felt little of his sexuality, had been far too intense, too hostile, too angry, to feel anything other than incensed hatred. She had wanted to punch out at him, to fight, to make him either give back the cottage or insist on seeing proof of possession. She had not wanted this delay, these few days; they had softened her feelings and she didn't *want* that, she wanted to remain angry with him.

Again she began to struggle but his hands slid from her shoulders—one to the small of her back, one between her shoulderblades—and he held her firmly against him. They were so close she could feel the steady beat of his heart—and her own unsteady response! His body was hard, packed with solid muscle, and his arms were like steel bands around her. There was no escape.

She looked up at him, her lips parted ready to protest, but before any words escaped his mouth came down on hers. It was not a savage kiss, not a brutal kiss, not a possessive kiss, as she had expected, not an assault; no, it was gentle, soft, sensual, persuasive. It was designed to draw out a total response—and it succeeded!

It was all and more than she had experienced in her dream. It was as though he had flicked on a switch and she had become alive, every tiny part of her sensitised, tingling, throbbing, *wanting*! It was unreal, this power he wielded over her. How or why she did not understand; all she knew was that suddenly she wanted his kiss.

Her tension turned to acquiescence, her body moved unconsciously against his, she parted her lips and his tongue touched and tasted and explored. Saira forgot where she was, forgot the circumstances, forgot Jarrett was her enemy, and returned his kiss with a passion that was alien to her. She had never kissed Tony like this, had never felt this frightening need, this longing to be possessed. She was shocked by it, it went against every principle she held, and with a surge of almost superhuman energy she wrenched herself free.

'Don't ever do that to me again,' she cried, her breast heaving as she fought for control.

Jarrett's lips curved into a mocking smile. 'Something tells me you're not as outraged as you pretend to be. I

have a feeling that you enjoyed the kiss, that you would
have liked to continue if it hadn't been for your sense
of outraged decency. I hadn't realised you were quite
such a prude.'

'There's a lot you don't know about me.' Her green
eyes flashed her anger and she tossed her hair off her
face in a defiant gesture.

'It will be interesting finding out.'

'That is something you'll never do,' she retorted coldly.
'Once this affair's sorted out you'll never see me again.'

'Are you conceding that Honeysuckle Cottage does
belong to me?' The humour was still there on his face,
mocking her, angering her, making her want to beat her
fists against his chest.

'I'm conceding nothing,' she snapped.

And still he smiled.

How could he remain so cool and unmoved? So totally
in charge of himself? Saira flashed him one last furious
glance before storming over to the door and yanking it
open. 'Goodnight, Mr Brent.'

'One day you'll call me Jarrett,' he said.

'Never!' she cried. 'I hate you, haven't you got the
message yet? You're anathema to me, and the less I see
of you, the better. In future I'll be in touch through my
aunt's solicitor.'

'Is this goodbye?' A sudden frown appeared, grooving
his brow, darkening his eyes.

'Yes, indeed.' Her chin came up, her eyes sparked. 'It
is best. I don't take kindly to being pawed by a stranger.
This is a business relationship, nothing more, forced on
me by circumstances beyond my control, and I resent
you trying to inflict yourself on me in other ways.'

'I thought I sensed a certain response?' He watched
her closely, the frown gone now, the infuriating smile

back in place. 'In fact, I not only thought it, I experi-enced it. My guess is that you frightened yourself with the depth of your feelings; that's what's making you run now.'

'I am not running away,' she cried. 'It's late, it's past midnight, I want to go to bed, I'm tired.' But damn him, he was right. He was too perceptive by far. She curled her fists as she stood in the doorway glowering.

'And when you get to the cottage you'll find you can't sleep, your mind will be too active going over and over the events of tonight. Isn't that right?'

'How the hell do I know?'

'Because it's the normal pattern when someone's upset or excited, and you seem to be both.'

'I am not upset,' she yelled.

'Excited, then?'

'Angry,' she tossed. 'And why the hell do you keep smiling? Am I so funny?'

'Not funny, beautiful; even more so when you're glaring like an enraged tigress.'

The deep timbre of his voice made the words sound like a caress and Saira felt a shiver of awareness rush through her. 'You're a hypocritical bast——'

'Saira!' Her words were abruptly cut off. 'That's no language for a lady.'

'I don't feel like a lady at this moment,' she retorted. 'I don't like being treated like this, and I——'

Again he stopped her. 'Treated like what, may I ask?' And there was a sudden hardening to his tone.

'As though I'm a possession,' she spat. 'Just because you've wined and dined me you seem to think it gives you some sort of right to make love. You're all the same, you men, you're selfish and arrogant and think of no one but yourselves.'

A frown divided his forehead at her harsh words. 'Maybe I am arrogant,' he declared, 'I'll admit to that, but selfish, no, that is the last thing I am.' He came across the room, his footsteps silent on the plain beige carpet, his eyes never leaving her face.

'I think it's yourself you're angry with, sweet Saira. You don't like to think that your body can respond to mine against your will. You like to be in control, and you probably always have been—especially where that boyfriend of yours was concerned.' His eyes dared her to deny it. 'But I'm different, and you resent it, and you resent the fact that there's a spark of awareness between us, a feeling that could, if you'd let it, develop into something more.'

Saira looked at him derisively. 'I think you're jumping to conclusions. I think you're seeing what you want to see.' But she was lying. Again, with him standing so close, her heart felt jittery, and she knew that if she didn't get away while she had the advantage there was a strong possibility of her staying the night.

Before he spoke again she managed to reach the front door and was congratulating herself on getting away without a further confrontation when he fell into step beside her. 'If you insist on going back to the cottage, the least I can do is escort you.'

'It doesn't matter,' she said, wildly shaking her head. 'I'll be fine.'

'But I wouldn't rest in my bed, wondering whether you were safe.'

Was that a hint of sarcasm? she wondered, at the same time protesting. 'No harm will come to me.'

'Probably not,' he agreed, 'but better safe than sorry, wouldn't you say?'

'Am I never to be rid of you?' she asked sharply.

'Your aunt would want me to look after you.'

It was a bright, moonlit night and Saira could see his face clearly. It had a bluish tinge, shining as though it were polished, and when she slanted him a glance she could see the inevitable smile. If anything was destined to rile her it was that.

'Maybe so,' she answered, 'but she certainly wouldn't want you to be a nuisance, which is what you are.' She hurried her steps and he kept pace at her side. She went even faster; he did the same. It was a ludicrous situation and she suddenly wanted to laugh, but knew that if she did it would dissolve the atmosphere between them, and who knew what would happen then. He was far too attractive for her peace of mind.

'Are we in a race?' The question was serious but she had a feeling that he saw the humorous side as well.

'If you had any conscience you'd know that I don't want you with me.'

'But I want you,' he muttered thickly, and his arm touched her elbow.

Saira tore herself away as if she had been burnt and almost ran the last few yards to the cottage. 'You can go back now,' she panted over her shoulder.

'Not until I've seen you safely inside,' he insisted.

And so she had to put up with him waiting patiently while she fumbled in her bag for her key and inserted it into the lock, and when she had trouble in turning it he stepped forward, 'Allow me,' and with a firm flick of his wrist he had the door open.

Before she could stop him he had stepped inside. 'What are you doing for light?'

'Nothing,' she said. 'I usually go to bed before it gets dark.'

'Have you no torch, candles, an oil lamp?'

'Not that I know of.'

'I think there is a lamp. Elizabeth used to have it lit in her window. If we're lucky it will still have some oil in. The best thing you can do is to stay here while I find it.'

He disappeared before she could protest, moving as easily through the small room as if he had nocturnal vision. Saira could hear him rummaging and finally she heard his exclamation of triumph. The next moment a match scraped and she saw a glimmer of light followed by a dull golden glow as he walked into the sitting-room with the lamp held aloft.

'Where did you find it?' she asked, as she could not remember seeing the lamp on her search of the house.

'On top of the dresser in the kitchen, along with a pile of other junk. There's so much that needs sorting out. Are you going to do it while you're here? I've been waiting for a member of the family to arrive and take charge of things.'

Saira eyed him cautiously. She wasn't sure that he was speaking the truth. 'And if no one had turned up?'

'I guess I would have disposed of the furniture, boxed everything else and held on to it, for a year or so at least.'

He was a difficult man to understand. At this moment he sounded thoughtful and caring, but she had also seen the arrogant, ruthless side of him, and as far as she was concerned these were the dominant traits. He'd had a soft spot for her aunt, admittedly, but he did not have one for her. He was playing with her, humiliating her, perhaps trying to crush her.

'I'm glad I've saved you the bother,' she said tightly, 'and now you've seen that I'm home safe and sound, you can go.'

'You seem to spend all your time turning me out,' he said with a harsh laugh.

'Doesn't that tell you something?' she spat.

'Oh, yes, it tells me that you don't want to be closely confined with me because you're scared witless of your own feelings.'

'I am not,' she cried indignantly. 'I have never been scared of how I feel in my life. I have always been in complete control of myself.'

'You're not now,' he told her brutally, 'and you don't like it, do you? Hence the defence barrier.'

'And how can you possibly know me?' she challenged. He was so uncannily accurate that she felt scared, but nevertheless she was determined to stand her ground.

He smiled slowly and easily. 'I've always prided myself on being a pretty good judge of character.'

'And you think that in the space of three days you know all about me?' The golden light made his tan look even deeper, made him more attractive, and she found it difficult to keep her eyes off him.

'Not everything,' he admitted, 'there's still a lot I'd like to know, but I think I'm beginning to get a good picture.'

'And so have I got a picture of you,' Saira riposted. 'Unfortunately it's not one I like. You're definitely not my type, Mr Jarrett Brent, and you'd do me a big favour if you got out of this cottage and out of my life right this very minute.'

'And if I refuse, what will you do, throw me out?'

'I would if I could,' she cried furiously, 'but as that's a physical impossibility, if you stay, I go. It's as simple as that.'

'You mean you'll give up your rights?'

'Damn you, no!' she exclaimed. 'Never, not until everything is sorted out legally, and I don't think even you will fail to respond to a solicitor's letter.' She was so angry she was quivering, and when Jarrett came towards her and enfolded her into his arms, holding her against him in a bearlike hug, she found, to her utter confusion, that she hadn't the strength to resist.

CHAPTER SIX

ON TUESDAY morning the skies were heavy and rain threatened. It had been oppressively warm during the night and Saira hoped against hope that they wouldn't have a storm. She hated storms; it was the one thing that fazed her. Even Aunt Lizzie, with her abundance of common sense, had not been able to persuade her that there was nothing to fear.

As she used the sparse, white bathroom later, as she splashed her face with cold water and brushed her teeth, she recalled the luxury in Jarrett's house and the harsh parallel of the situation made her angry. It was unfair that one man should have so much and yet still insist that this cottage was his as well.

Last night she had come very close to actually liking Jarrett Brent. When he had held her in his arms just before he left it was no sexual embrace—much to her surprise, it was calming and soothing, and when he felt her relax he had immediately let her go, not pressing home his advantage. 'Goodnight, my fiery Saira,' was all he had said.

But now, in the cold, clear light of day, she did not see it as gentlemanly behaviour, she saw it as strategy, another phase in the game he was playing—and her anger deepened.

As she brushed her hair, more viciously than usual, and fixed it into its regular plait, Saira wondered whether the postman had been to the Hall yet, whether Jarrett Brent had received Mr Kirby's letter. And she suddenly remembered that she must telephone her mother, must let her know that she intended staying longer than she had originally planned.

To her frustration the public telephone was out of order. It was unthinkable to go up to the Hall and ask Jarrett if she could use his, the Challoner's Arms wasn't yet open, and she didn't wish to intrude on any of the neighbours. She didn't suppose for one minute that Mrs Edistone would mind, but she would unashamedly listen to her conversation and everyone in the village would know her business. With a bit of luck perhaps the telephone would be mended by the end of the day.

As she walked back to the cottage Saira wondered what Jarrett Brent would do about Mr Kirby's letter. Would he send a copy of the deeds, saying he had them, to the solicitor, or bring them straight to her? And how long would it take him? Would he do it today, this morning, this afternoon? He seemed to be playing some sort of waiting game, enjoying the fact that he was holding her up. If he produced his proof promptly she could be back home in Darlington this evening and there would be no need to telephone her mother.

It suddenly struck her that she was perilously close to accepting the fact that Honeysuckle Cottage did actually belong to Jarrett Brent, and the thought appalled her. She was out of her mind; the cottage was hers, hers alone. He had no right to it. She mustn't think this way, it was dangerous.

She quickened her steps as her anger fuelled itself, and when she marched back into the cottage and found her enemy comfortably ensconced in her sitting-room she nearly exploded. 'What the hell do you think you're doing? How did you get in?'

He pushed himself lazily up from the armchair, his infuriating smile very much in evidence. He wore a pair of navy trousers and a white, open-necked shirt, and he looked fresh and alert, and very, very sexy! 'You left your door unlocked. I thought you'd be interested in looking at this.' He waved a large, brown manila envelope in front of her face.

The deeds! Saira felt as if her heart had dropped into her shoes. He was offering her irrefutable proof. This was the end of her dream. *She* was the one who was trespassing.

With reluctance she took it from him and her stomach turned uneasily as she reached out a sheet of paper. She glanced briefly at the contents and then looked at him with a sharp frown. 'This isn't the deeds.'

'Isn't it proof enough?'

'It's an agreement between you and my aunt, yes, saying that she's going to transfer the cottage into your name, but who's to say it's legal?'

'I do.'

'And I am supposed to take your word when you wouldn't take mine?' Saira's green eyes flashed her fury. 'Where are the deeds? They are what count.'

'I do not have them in my possession, not at the moment.'

'Your estate manager?'

'That's right.'

'He's still ill?'

'In Intensive Care, I'm afraid. I can't bother him with such trivialities at the moment.' He smiled as he spoke, the inevitable, infuriating smile, convincing Saira yet again that he was not speaking the truth; that although his estate manager might well be ill, he could easily lay his hands on the deeds if he wanted to, that for reasons known only to himself he was stalling.

'I don't happen to think it's trivial,' she retorted coldly. 'It's the most important thing in my life at the moment. I love this cottage, I've always loved it, and the fact that Aunt Lizzie left it to me proved that she took my love into account. I'll show this to Mr Kirby,' she said coldly, putting the document back into its envelope. 'We'll see what he has to say.'

It had gone quite dark as they spoke and now it began to rain, a sudden, heavy downpour that bounced off the old flagstones, that lashed the windows, that ran off the roof—but so far no thunder! Saira mentally crossed her fingers that there would be none.

'I trust you're not going to follow your usual pattern and throw me out?' Jarrett's deep blue eyes glinted and Saira felt like taking a swipe at him.

'Nothing would give me more pleasure,' she hissed.

'But you wouldn't be so cruel at a time like this,' he assumed. 'How about a cup of coffee to pass the time?'

Saira glared. 'Unless you can produce heat out of nothing you'll have to settle for cold milk or water.'

An expression she could not quite fathom flitted over his face; it could have been guilt, it could have been glee. He lifted his wide shoulders. 'I guess I forgot for a moment that you're living spartanly.'

'Forgot?' queried Saira harshly. Lord, did he really expect her to believe that?

'It slipped my mind; you seem so comfortable. You've not had a hot breakfast, then?'

'I've not had *any* breakfast,' she retorted. 'I went out to ring my mother before she went to work but the stupid phone was out of order.'

'My!' He lifted his thick brows reprovingly. 'We are in a bad mood this morning.'

'I only have to look at you and I'm in a bad mood,' she snapped. 'You spell trouble, Mr Brent, trouble with a capital T. I wish I'd never set eyes on you.' She was nettled because he'd actually produced proof—of some sort—when she'd hoped that he would be unable to do so.

She was disappointed, hurt, upset; she was hungry, it was raining, *he* was here; it looked as if she'd lost her battle. All these things heaped one on top of the other and she wanted to lash out, she wanted to bang her fists, she wanted to scream, to shout, to vent her fury—and he was in the firing line. And suddenly a clap of thunder added to her misery.

She shuddered and clapped her hands to her ears, closing her eyes, wanting to rush and hide somewhere safe. Instantly Jarrett Brent closed the gap between them, his arms came about her, and she was held in a protective embrace.

One half of her wanted to fight him off, the other, more fearful half wanted to curl into the shelter he was offering. And when a second or two later another burst of thunder reverberated through the skies she clung to him passionately.

When her trembling subsided he led her to the couch, sitting in the corner himself and curving her into him, both arms around her, murmuring words of comfort— much as her aunt had done years ago! The feelings were very different. Although she was scared witless, although she appreciated him trying to allay her fears, almost overriding these feelings was her awareness of Jarrett Brent, the man. Mingled with her shivers of terror were shivers of pleasure.

With each clap of thunder his arms tightened, his hands soothed, his voice comforted; her head nestled into the crook of his arm, he covered her ears, he stroked her hair. Time ceased to exist—and she had the strange thought that if Jarrett Brent were with her always she would never be so afraid of storms again.

She dismissed it instantly because it was a futile thought. For one thing she hated him—even though she felt a reluctant physical attraction; and another, it would never happen because of his relationship with Joy. Whatever he said, Saira was still of the impression that they were a couple. He might be playing the field but he would end up going back to Joy, she felt sure about that.

The storm gradually moved away but still he held her, and Saira herself was reluctant to move; not even in Tony's arms had she felt so safe, so relaxed. Until he said, 'Would you like to telephone your mother from the Hall?' and she remembered that he was the enemy.

She shook her head and struggled to get up. 'No, thank you.'

His mouth tightened at the coldness in her tone. 'Won't she be worried about you?'

Saira finally got to her feet. 'She'll be at work now.'

'Tonight, then, you can ring her.'

Saira eyed him coldly. 'I'll make my own plans, thank you.' She did not tell him that she had hoped to be home tonight and now he had squashed all hope of that. And if it hadn't been still raining she would have thrown open the door and asked him to leave. If he'd had his car, even, she would have done so, but he was apparently on foot and it was raining so heavily that no one with any sense would venture out.

She moved through into the kitchen, and he followed. She tipped some cornflakes into a bowl, sprinkled them with sugar and poured on the milk, and he stood watching. 'Would you like some?' she asked ungraciously.

Jarrett shook his head. 'I've already eaten. Gibbs cooked me bacon and sausage and mushroom and tomatoes and egg. And to follow I had toast and——'

'Oh, shut up,' cut in Saira fiercely. 'If you're trying to make me jealous you're succeeding.'

'You could leave that and come back with me for a proper cooked breakfast.'

Saira could just imagine Mrs Dour's reaction if she was asked to cook all over again. This wasn't her beloved Jarrett but a girl she had taken an instant dislike to. She would probably burn the bacon and fry her egg to a crisp. 'I wouldn't dream of putting your housekeeper to so much trouble,' she said haughtily. 'In any case, I like cornflakes, I really do.'

'You're the loser,' he said, and she could see he wasn't happy at her rejection.

'Why don't you go and sit in the other room,' she said, when he continued to watch her eat.

'And miss out on the fire and brimstone? You're a delight, Saira. There's certainly never a dull moment when I'm with you.'

'You like amusing yourself at my expense?' Brilliant green eyes flashed across the tiny room.

'Not strictly, not when I'm in the firing line, but you're an exhilaration. I've never met a girl quite like you before.'

'Then we're equals.' She eyed him proudly and savagely.

'Doesn't that give us some type of bond?' The mocking humour was there again and if anything was guaranteed to irritate her it was this.

'You have to be joking,' she cried. 'I have no wish to be associated with you in any way whatsoever.'

'So you keep saying.'

'So why don't you take the hint?'

A muscle jerked in his jaw though the smile was still in place. 'I'm here regarding the cottage, in case you'd forgotten. You were anxious to find out whether I was speaking the truth.'

'And now it's the weather that's detaining you?' she asked drily.

'I'm afraid so.'

'You could borrow one of Aunt Lizzie's umbrellas.'

'Not likely,' he barked. 'I've seen Elizabeth's umbrella collection. She had a quirky taste in that direction; the brighter and gaudier the better. Can you imagine me walking through the village carrying something like that?'

It painted a ludicrous picture and Saira could not help smiling. 'It would be highly entertaining.'

'And ruin my reputation.'

'That wouldn't worry me,' she announced.

'You're a little minx, do you know that?' he growled. 'I think I ought to put you over my knee and give you the spanking you deserve.'

'Oh, yes, you and who else?' jeered Saira, and then wished she hadn't when he walked purposefully around the well-scrubbed kitchen table, catching hold of her wrist and pulling her to her feet.

Unsure whether he was serious or just testing her Saira began to struggle. 'You dare,' she cried, 'you just dare.'

The next moment his mouth found hers. 'Oh, I dare all right, my lady,' he muttered, 'but I think I prefer this sort of punishment.'

Like all his other kisses it sent her senses into panic, especially coming so close on the heels of his earlier embrace—even though that had been entirely without sexual connotations. There was a sense of urgency about him now, as though her taunting had incited him, and when he breathed against her lips, 'This is an infinitely preferable sort of breakfast,' she had to agree with him.

The kiss seemed to last forever. Not only did he explore her mouth, but the rest of her face too, and she felt him pulling at the band in her hair until he had it free, until he eased her braid apart and then, running both hands through it, brought her hair forward in a shower of corn-coloured silk about her face.

He paused a moment to admire it, to simply stroke her hair, and then he cupped her face with his palms and kissed her all over again.

By this time Saira was beginning to lose control. He was the most sensual man she had ever met and it was impossible to resist him. She felt breathless, powerless, under some sort of spell, and when his hand moved to cup her breast through the thin cotton of her T-shirt, letting it nestle in his hand and stroking his thumb over the already hardened nub, she wriggled against him, a tiny moan of satisfaction escaping the back of her throat.

Her heart thumped and every part of her body became sensitised; she closed her eyes and felt an ache of desire in her groin. It was not until he attempted to pull her T-shirt out of her jeans that she demurred. She gave a tiny jerk, as though she had just woken. 'No, Jarrett.'

To her amazement he stopped, and there was a delighted smile on his face. 'Do you realise what you've just said?'

Saira frowned faintly and shook her head. 'I said no, but——'

'You called me Jarrett. Now wouldn't you say that was a step in the right direction? Wouldn't you say that this morning we've crossed a barrier? Hell, I love your hair.' He lifted it again, letting it slide through his fingers, gazing at it reverently, holding it up to his face and smelling its freshness.

Saira herself was unaware that she had said his name and she wanted to back away now, but this was an appreciation she had never encountered before and it was heady stuff. More than one person had told her that she had beautiful hair, but they had never revered it to this extent. His very genuine admiration was as intoxicating as his kisses. She watched his face, saw the expression that went beyond anything she had encountered before, and felt as though she was being made love to.

Without conscious thought Saira put her hands on his arms, wanting him to hold her again, wanting to feel his strength against her. He looked into her shining eyes and still with her hair entwined through his fingers pulled her face close to his.

'Is this what you want?' he muttered thickly, his mouth brushing hers lightly, erotically, sending a clamour of feeling from the back of her aching throat right down to the very pit of her stomach.

She nodded briefly, closing her eyes, giving herself up to the pleasure of the moment. It was a long, slow, sensual kiss, his lips and tongue tasting, exploring, inciting. Saira ground her hips against him, opening her mouth willingly to his, responding freely, feeling no inhibitions whatsoever.

She wanted him to touch her breasts again as he had a few moments earlier, she actually felt herself aching for his touch, but this time he held himself well in check, concentrating his assault on her mouth, kissing her in ways no other man ever had, seeming to find intense pleasure in kissing just the corner of her mouth, or the soft skin inside her lower lip, treating each part as an extra delicacy. When he put her from him she felt acutely disappointed. She wanted the kiss to go on for ever.

'Your boyfriend was a fool for letting you go.'

His words, though softly spoken, were enough to jolt Saira back to reality. What was she doing? Why was she letting this man kiss her? And more shamefully still, how could she have instigated this last kiss? She did not want a relationship of this sort with Jarrett, with any man for that matter. None of them were to be trusted. Goodness, she must be out of her mind. She snatched away from him, her eyes wide and distressed.

'Are you having regrets?' He looked at her with a frown creasing his brow, his whole attitude one of puzzlement.

Saira felt confused by the strength of her emotions. Her body still tingled, she felt disorientated. They were sensations that were alien to her, especially after a single kiss. What was happening? 'You're damn right I'm having regrets,' she stormed. 'You had no right taking advantage of me like that.'

'Taking advantage?' He gave a bark of cheerless laughter. 'Think again, Saira; you were as eager as I.'

'If I was, I was a fool,' she snapped. 'I let myself get carried away in the heat of the moment. I don't want any of this, I don't want your kisses; keep them for Joy, she's the one you should be giving them to.'

'But Joy's not here and you are.'

'And that's as much as you care, isn't it?' she demanded. 'You're willing to take your pleasure with any girl? "Joy won't mind, Joy and I have an understanding, Joy and I have an open relationship, I can do what I like." Is that your philosophy?'

His mouth tightened. 'It's what you seem to think it is.'

'And you're not denying it?'

'Would you believe me if I did?' His eyes were hard on hers.

'I doubt it,' Saira retorted sharply.

'So what's the point?' he asked. 'I'm already judged and found guilty.'

'That's right,' she said, and glancing away from him to the window, 'I do believe it's stopped raining.'

'Is that my cue to leave?'

'You bet it is,' she said.

'What are your plans for the rest of the day? The offer's still on if you'd like to go riding?'

She looked at him sharply. 'I don't think so. I'm naturally going to see Mr Kirby this morning, and then I intend sorting through my aunt's possessions.'

'And how are you going to get to Mr Kirby's office? It's in Ripon, I believe.'

Saira lifted her shoulders. 'I don't know; bus, taxi, or whatever. I'll find some way.'

'I'm not even sure there is a bus service in the village any longer,' he said, 'and if there is you can bet your bottom dollar that it won't be convenient for your purpose; and a taxi will cost you a small fortune. I can give you a lift if you like?'

Saira did not like, she did not want to spend any more time with this man, it was far too easy to give in to him. 'No, thank you,' she answered brittly. 'I'll take a taxi. Perhaps you would order one for me when you go home?'

'If you're sure?' He looked displeased by her request. 'It would be no trouble at all for me to——'

'I am perfectly sure,' Saira told him firmly. 'I want no favours from you.' All she wanted was her cottage.

Mr Kirby had a client with him and Saira had to wait almost an hour. Her own fault for not making an appointment, she thought resignedly, as she accepted a second cup of tea from his receptionist.

When finally she did get in to see him, he studied the agreement very carefully. 'This certainly looks like your aunt's handwriting, but if we're to take this as proof then I would need to get it verified by an expert. You've not come across the deeds?'

Saira shook her head. 'I've looked everywhere.'

'And this man, this Jarrett Brent, he hasn't produced any deeds either?'

'He claims that they're filed away in his agent's office,' said Saira, 'but that he can't get his hands on them until the man comes back, and as he's very ill at the moment it's likely to be a long time. Actually I don't believe him.'

Mr Kirby frowned. He was a grey-haired man of her aunt's era with a full face of whiskers and a ruddy complexion. 'That is not good enough.'

'I agree, but it's the best I can get out of him,' she replied. 'He wanted me to accept this agreement instead.'

'Leave this with me,' said Mr Kirby fiercely. 'The matter calls for stiffer action, a court order if necessary.'

Saira grimaced. 'But that will take time, I was hoping it would be cleared up quickly. I have to go home; I can't take more than a week off.'

He looked at her wryly. 'I'll do my best, I'll give the matter my immediate and personal attention, but a week is hardly long enough. I can see no point in your hanging around waiting. Why don't you go home and I'll get in touch with you just as soon as I have any news?'

Saira left his office feeling no happier than when she arrived. She ate lunch in a café in Ripon and then took another taxi back to Amplethwaite. Once back at Honeysuckle Cottage she changed into her jeans and with grim determination set about dividing her aunt's stuff into what she wanted to keep and what was fit only to be burnt.

When she had looked through it before she had been intent only on finding the deeds, now it took her much longer. Everything had to be inspected: papers, ornaments, linen, pictures, furniture, clothes. She soon realised it would take her more than one afternoon, probably for the rest of the week! And she had barely got going when a light tap sounded on the door. Of one thing she was sure, it was definitely not Jarrett; his knock was loud and demanding. It was probably Mrs Edistone come to satisfy her curiosity.

To Saira's surprise it not her elderly neighbour either but Joy Woodstock who stood there, and the pleasant smile that had been painted on her face in the restaurant last night was conspicuous by its absence.

'Do come in,' said Saira, even though she knew instinctively that the girl's visit was not a social one. 'I'm afraid the place is in a bit of a mess because——'

'What I have to say I'll say here,' retorted Joy haughtily. 'I want to know what your intentions are as far as Jarrett is concerned?'

'My intentions?' Saira gave an uncomfortable laugh. 'I don't have any, I'm afraid. Jarrett doesn't——'

'That isn't what it looks like to me,' cut in the dark-haired girl fiercely. 'The two of you looked very cosy last night and I want to tell you right here and now that he's mine. I love Jarrett and intend to marry him; I'm not letting him go. I know he's always had an eye for other girls, but believe me I'm the one he always comes back to, I'm the one who he's going to spend the rest of his life with.'

The woman's attitude irritated Saira beyond measure. 'I think Jarrett should decide that for himself,' she said, letting a coolly confident smile play about her lips.

Joy sniffed deprecatingly. 'You might think he's in love with you, but it won't last. I've seen it all before.'

'It strikes me,' said Saira, resenting her officious attitude, 'that if he truly was in love with you he wouldn't be interested in other girls.'

'He does love me,' Joy stated firmly, 'and I love him, and if you know what's good for you you'll back off now before you get hurt.'

She was so tiny yet so uptight that Saira wanted to laugh. She was a spirited little thing without a doubt, and she couldn't help but admire her courage in coming here today. 'I'll bear that in mind,' she said.

Joy looked at her suspiciously as if suspecting that she wasn't serious. 'Just make sure that you do.' And with a further glare, a further toss of her immaculate black hair, she retreated down the path and climbed into her red sports car. The wheels spun as she accelerated quickly away.

There goes one very unhappy woman, thought Saira. But really Joy need not have worried. Jarrett wasn't serious in his pursuit of her, and he was the last man on earth she wanted a serious relationship with. Joy was welcome to him. She turned back to her sorting.

There was one place she hadn't looked before, and that was on top of the dresser in the kitchen where Jarrett had found the lamp. She climbed on a stool and peered. To her amazement there was quite an assortment, all hidden from view down below. A pair of ornate brass candlesticks that looked as though they might be worth a lot of money: a jade Buddha, a richly gilded Royal Worcester vase, a silver jewellery casket, a small metal safe, as well as lots of other smaller ornaments.

This must have been Aunt Lizzie's hiding place, she thought, where she had put all her most valuable and treasured possessions before leaving for the States. And the house had lain empty all those months! Anyone could have got in and taken whatever they liked and no one would have been any the wiser. It didn't bear thinking about.

It was the safe that interested her most. Somewhere she had seen some keys which hadn't fitted anything. Saira racked her brains; yes, that was it, in the cutlery drawer right here in the kitchen. Not a very unique hiding place.

Soon she had the small box open and inside were two official-looking envelopes. She picked up the first one. Could it be what she was looking for? Her heart hammered as she took out the contents and discovered, not the deeds, as she had half-hoped, but a will, a will revoking all other wills, a will dated just before her aunt died!

CHAPTER SEVEN

SAIRA felt her spirits sink lower and lower as she read the contents of Aunt Lizzie's will. There was no mention of Honeysuckle Cottage, merely a list of her possessions to be divided out fairly between her relatives. Saira was to get the Royal Worcester vase, some of her jewellery, her Victorian bedroom furniture, and a share of whatever money there was.

It looked as though Jarrett Brent had been right all along; Aunt Lizzie had sold to him and Mr Kirby had not been informed. Saira was naturally disappointed over the cottage but even more devastated at the thought that her aunt had been in such dire straits that she had been forced to sell. Why hadn't she told them? Why hadn't she said anything? Why had she done this thing all alone?

Saira's thoughts were many and muddled; she was upset by the fact that her aunt had been compelled to give up her home of so many years, and could not help wondering whether it had really been necessary, or whether Jarrett Brent had talked her into it. The thought would not go away because surely, if Aunt Lizzie had been in financial trouble, she would have told her family? They were close, they always had been; she wouldn't have kept something like this from them.

She folded the will and put it back into its envelope. There was not a lot she could do. It was all over now, Jarrett was right and she was wrong. She would desperately hate having to admit it after the way she had behaved—but what choice had she? She could just im-

106

agine the look on his face, the I-told-you-so expression, and she gritted her teeth.

When Saira picked up the other envelope she did not expect to find anything else of such vital importance, and was therefore completely stunned when she came across the actual official papers detailing the sale of the cottage—to a Mr Jarrett Armstrong-Brent.

Armstrong-Brent! The name rang loud warning bells in Saira's head. She was transported back ten years, to the time her father suffered a fatal heart attack because they were being forced out of their rented Victorian terraced house in which he had lived all his life.

Memories were vivid. Tall, frightening William Armstrong-Brent, the man at the head of the firm of developers, a man with fierce, bristling eyebrows, a hard, chiselled face and compelling navy eyes; darker than Jarrett's, but with the same intense power—obviously Jarrett's father!

He had banged on the door and walked into their house and threatened them with dire consequences if they did not get out. Everyone else in the street had moved; they were the only family to dig their heels well and truly in.

Saira had been extremely frightened, but she also had not liked the way he spoke to her parents and she had run across the room and hit him with her fists, telling him to go away and leave them alone.

He had called her a spitfire and taken not the least bit of notice, and it was after he had gone that her father had suffered his first near-fatal heart attack. The second one had come with the trauma of the move. Saira had never forgotten the day her mother told her that her father was dead.

And she could not help thinking now that Jarrett might have done the same to her aunt. Perhaps that was why she had gone to America? Perhaps that was why she had died? All they knew was that she had suffered a heart attack—could it have stemmed back to his harassing her about the cottage?

Suddenly and feverishly Saira hated him more than ever, and was so angry with herself for having been taken in, for letting him see that she was attracted to him, that she could not keep a limb still.

She wanted to go up to the Hall straight away and vent her fury on Jarrett *Armstrong*-Brent, but her innate sense of fairness told her that she had to get back to Mr Kirby with the will first, before he sent his harsh letter to Jarrett.

This time she went to the village shop and asked them to call her a taxi and while waiting changed back into her dress and high heels. She made it about half an hour before Mr Kirby was due to close for the day, and ten minutes before the mail went.

Mr Kirby was as surprised as Saira by the discovery of another will and could not believe that Elizabeth had said nothing to him. 'Unless it's because she knew I wouldn't approve of her selling her home,' he said. 'It's going to take time to sort out. I'll have to verify that it's genuine and legal and then apply for new probate. I'll also have to try to recover the money that's already been handed out, because some of it is now yours.'

'Goodness, that doesn't matter,' cried Saira. 'I wouldn't dream of taking it back off anyone; that would be most unfair. What concerns me is ownership of the cottage, and it would appear that my aunt did sell to Jarrett Brent after all.'

Mr Kirby had to agree that it did seem to be the case. 'I will, of course, still be in touch with him and ask for confirmation that the deeds are in his name. I'm sorry, Saira, it must be very upsetting for you.'

Saira grimaced. 'Very. I never knew she was so badly off that she had to sell.'

'You'll definitely be going home now, I take it?' It was a gentle, concerned question. Mr Kirby was as distressed as Saira by the turn of events.

She nodded. There was nothing left for her here, except to go and see Jarrett Brent for one last time, and boy, would she give him a piece of her mind.

'I'll be in touch as soon as everything is sorted out.' Mr Kirby told her.

It had been a good dream while it lasted, she thought, as the taxi headed back; she had even begun to think that she might like to live here permanently. Now all such thoughts were dashed completely; all she could think of was the snake in the grass who had swindled her aunt out of her home.

As they drove through the narrow village street Saira saw Jarrett's white Mercedes parked outside the cottage. She could not think why he was there but at least it brought the confrontation forward, and her blood boiled as she prepared herself for the attack. She paid off the taxi driver and turned to face Jarrett as he swung easily out of his car.

'I didn't expect you to be away this long,' he said, by way of greeting.

'I didn't know you were keeping tabs on me,' she retorted, as she unlocked the cottage door. 'What are you doing here?'

His smile faded at the harshness of her reply. 'I actually came to tell you that I've arranged to have the

electricity put back on, the telephone reconnected too.'
He followed her inside.

Saira eyed him scornfully. If he expected her to thank
him he was mistaken. 'And I'm supposed to think that's
very considerate of you, am I?'

He looked at her in sudden surprise. 'What's wrong?
Did everything not go to your satisfaction? What did
Mr Kirby have to say?'

'There have been further developments,' she told him
abruptly.

'And I take it they're not to your liking?'

'Indeed they're not,' she snapped, 'although I suppose
it's no more than I should have expected.'

He frowned, then said, 'I think you should sit down.
You look as though you're in a state of shock.'

'To put it mildly,' riposted Saira, and led the way into
the kitchen where the objects she had found on top of
the dresser were still laid out on the table. Predominant
was the now empty safe box.

Jarrett's eyes were drawn immediately to it, his thick
brows rising, and he sat down on one of the old kitchen
stools and waited.

Saira sat too. 'First things first,' she said, her chin
high. 'It would appear I've misjudged you.'

Jarrett's brows lifted in surprise, then his lips quirked
annoyingly. 'That's a mighty big concession coming from
you.'

'Made only because I've found out the truth,' she said
heatedly. 'My aunt left another will, I found it in that
box.' Her eyes were fierce as she looked at him. 'Yes,
the cottage is yours, and you'll be pleased to hear that
I'm going home and won't be bothering you again.'

She sensed rather than saw his sudden tension, but his
frown was very real, drawing his brows tightly together.

'I took it to Mr Kirby,' she said.

'And?'

'And nothing, that's the end of it.'

'So now you're leaving?' There was a stillness about him that she found unnerving.

'Yes.'

'This has come as a great surprise.'

'You don't really expect me to believe that, do you?' she asked savagely. 'You've kept insisting that the cottage is yours, you've wanted me out, and now you've got your wish. I don't actually believe my aunt's sale of the cottage was as straightforward as you make out, but that will wait. I'll get to the bottom of it one day.' She paused and drew breath. 'There is one other thing I want to say before I go, something that's upset me even more than the discovery that you're the real owner of this cottage.'

His head jerked and he looked at her sharply. 'And that is?' he asked, still faintly frowning.

She pushed herself up from her chair, her whole body trembling with anger. 'It's something your father did that's upsetting me—no, not upsetting, that's too mild a word. I'm furious.' Her eyes flashed, her whole body sent out messages of rejection.

His eyes narrowed at mention of his father and he rose too. 'Now you have me completely confused. What has my father got to do with all this?' His words were clipped, his tone brusque, his long fingers drumming on the edge of the table.

Saira eyed him coldly and condemningly for a few seconds, and he held her gaze, and she felt nothing at all for him except contempt and anger. Not disappointment, not regret for what might have been, nothing except stone cold fury. '*Your* father killed *my* father,' she stated flatly.

He could not have been more shocked had she declared that the end of the world was near. He shook his head, fiercely repudiating her accusation. 'That's ridiculous. How can you make such a statement? My father never killed anyone in his life, not even a fly; he wasn't the type.'

Saira snorted indelicately. 'But he was a hard businessman?'

'I guess so,' he admitted, 'I am myself. It's a rat race out there, every man for himself.'

'At the expense of someone else's life?' she blazed.

'By someone else you mean your father?' Jarrett's confusion changed to anger. 'How dare you make such an accusation. What grounds do you have? Slander is a very serious crime, do you realise that?' A muscle jerked in his jaw now, his whole body stiffened, and his eyes were hard upon hers.

'I know exactly what I'm talking about,' Saira retorted furiously.

'Then you'd better tell me,' he snarled.

Her green eyes were icily condemning. 'My father died as a result of your father kicking him out of his house.' She spoke slowly and clearly and waited for his reaction, and could not believe it when Jarrett laughed, even though it was harsh and held no humour. 'I see nothing funny in the situation,' she flashed.

'You're making a mountain out of a molehill, Saira.' His anger had abated somewhat and he sought to touch her, but she backed away as though afraid of being contaminated. He frowned grimly. 'I don't know the circumstances, but I do know that my father would never harass someone to that extent. Where did you get this information from all of a sudden?'

'I found out that your real name is *Armstrong*-Brent and it was William Armstrong-Brent, of Armstrongs the developers, who hounded my father to his death. William was your father, I presume?' It was too unusual a surname for it to be anyone else.

Jarrett inclined his head.

'And did you drop the Armstrong because you were ashamed of your father's shady deeds?' Saira was actually trembling in her anger, unable to keep a limb still, moving from foot to foot, glaring, loathing, wishing she had never set eyes on this man.

'I dropped it because I thought that a double-barrelled surname was too pretentious,' he told her, 'not that I expect you to believe that in your present frame of mind.'

'You're dead right, I don't,' she spat. 'I'll never believe anything you tell me again. And now I've had my say I want you to get out and leave me to pack in peace.'

'I'd like to have my say.' There was a coldness in his eyes that made her shiver. 'I will not condone unfounded accusations against my father.

'Unfounded?' she shrieked. 'Your father came to our house threatening us because we were the only ones in the street who wouldn't move—he was going to build a business park or something in the area—and he was so high-handed about the whole thing that my father had a heart attack as soon as he left.'

'I am sorry,' said Jarrett, 'but my father cannot be held responsible for the state of your father's health.'

Saira snorted angrily. 'And when we finally moved, when William Armstrong-Brent——' she spat the name as though it were poison '—*forced* us out, my father had another, fatal heart attack. How can you say that had nothing to do with him?'

Jarrett drew in a harsh breath and remained silent for several seconds. 'There must be many people in this world,' he said at length, 'who have suffered heart attacks as a result of highly emotive circumstances, but in no instance can another person be held completely responsible.'

Saira's eyes flashed. 'Rubbish! I cannot accept that. Have you any idea at all how I felt when my father died? He was forty-six, he should have lived at least another thirty years. He would have been alive now if it hadn't been for your father.'

But she knew she was fighting a losing battle. She could argue the issue all day long and Jarrett would never agree that his father had indirectly caused Graham Carlton's death. She suddenly felt cold, rubbing her upper arms, shivering, wanting nothing more at this moment than to walk out of the cottage and out of Jarrett Brent's life for ever. 'Please go,' she said, her voice almost a whisper.

'I know how you feel, Saira,' said Jarrett, shaking his head, and his tone was quieter too, 'but there is something I need to say.'

'Nothing you can say will make any difference,' she said tiredly.

'It's not about my father, or yours,' he said, and, after a slight pause, 'It's about the cottage.'

Saira frowned. Now what? She was too tired for any more arguments today.

'I want you to have it.'

Her head jerked back on her shoulders. This was the last thing she had expected. 'To appease your conscience?' she cried. Lord, he was insensitive. 'No, thank you very much. It's yours—you keep it.'

'Lizzie wanted you to have it.'

Saira frowned and looked at him sharply. 'You said Lizzie never mentioned me so how could you know? Or was that yet another lie? Did she discuss me?'

Jarrett shook his head. 'No, she didn't. But if she left this cottage to you in her original will it must have been what she really wanted; therefore I'd like you to have it.'

Extremely suspicious of his motives now, Saira eyed him with distaste. 'There has to be some catch. All along you've insisted this cottage is yours, and now, when it's finally been proved, you're prepared to give it up. I don't understand.' She shook her head as she spoke. 'Or was it that you *persuaded* her she should sell? Maybe she did it against her will?' And now he was offering it back to her because he felt guilty.

A harsh frown jagged his brow. 'Exactly what are you suggesting?' The anger was back with a vengeance.

Her chin lifted and she eyed him coldly. 'I believe you've bought quite a lot of property around here. Rumour has it that you want to own the entire village.'

A look of pure outrage crossed his face. 'Rumour has it wrong. Whoever told you that is a liar.' He paced the room, calming himself with difficulty, finally turning back to her. 'It's pure speculation, Saira, by people who have nothing better to do. I'm a property developer, I buy property, but I do not force people out of their homes. Now let that be an end to it.'

As far as Saira was concerned it wasn't the end, but she saw the folly of trying to argue with him further at this stage, so she retained her silence and, after a further few minutes struggling with himself, Jarrett said, 'We were talking about the cottage.'

'Yes.' Saira half expected him to say that he had changed his mind. It had been an unexpected proposal anyway, and one she was inclined to throw back in his face.

'I still want you to have it.' And suddenly there was the suspicion of a smile on his lips. 'If you hadn't been so hoity-toity when you first came, so ready to doubt me, I might have conceded then. As it was, I was incensed by you casting aspersions on my character.'

'You mean you were prepared to admit right from the beginning that Honeysuckle Cottage should rightfully be mine?' Saira eyed him guardedly, not altogether sure whether she believed him even now.

'Not exactly,' he admitted, 'but I was prepared to give it up—solely because I was very fond of your aunt and wanted her wishes to be carried out.'

'That was very charitable of you,' conceded Saira, but it was clear by her tone that she still doubted him.

Jarrett frowned. 'You don't believe me?'

'As a matter of fact, no.' Her eyes were bold upon his.

'It's the truth,' he assured her, 'only your attitude stopped me. So, Saira, are you going to accept?'

Saira was torn. Lord, she still hated him, she hated what his family had done to hers, and she hated the way he had played with her these last few days. It would appease her sense of justice if she did accept his offer. He deserved to lose it after the way he had behaved, but would she be happy living here now?

She still foolishly felt a strong physical attraction towards Jarrett, not that she expected it to develop into anything stronger; he was a powerful and dangerous man to tangle with, she was best keeping her distance. Both his and his father's track records were hardly recommendations for a peaceful and joyous relationship.

'I'm waiting,' he said quietly.

'I have a job in Darlington,' Saira prevaricated.

He shook his head, dismissing her excuse out of hand. 'You can get one here. In any case, it's not really too far; many people travel thirty miles to work, or even more; I see no problem. You'll have to get a car, of course, but——'

'I have a car at home,' she interjected, not wanting him to think she was strictly bereft. She failed to mention that it was old and not very reliable.

'Then you have no excuse.'

'Maybe I don't want to move.'

His eyes narrowed. 'Then why were you so keen on getting your hands on this house?'

'I'd probably have used it as a holiday home,' she answered with a slight shrug.

'You didn't intend settling here permanently?' A harsh frown suddenly creased his brow.

Saira twisted her lips. 'I have thought about it,' she admitted reluctantly.

He smiled. 'So—there's no problem.' He moved a step closer towards her. 'I suggest you put off your return and come and have supper with me. You can ring your mother while you're there, if you didn't do so when you were in Ripon, and we can iron out the details of the cottage.'

Saira wished he would move away, she could not think straight when he stood so near. Her whole body reacted to his and her mind grew confused.

'Well, Saira?'

To her annoyance she found herself nodding.

'Good.' He looked pleased. 'I'll leave you to get ready; come up about seven.'

When he had gone Saira drew in a much-needed breath. His presence had been claustrophobic, the air thick with tension and anger and hatred; it had been the most enervating half-hour of her life. She slumped back down on her seat, her mind a maelstrom of emotions.

Jarrett had offered to give her the cottage! She had promised to go up there for supper and talk about it! Was she in her right mind? How could she accept such an offer from the enemy? Why had he made it in the first place?

There had to be some devious reason, some cunning motive, but what? Would it be wise to stay, to accept, to make her home here after what she had just found out? Could she stand being beholden to him in this manner?

She glanced at her watch: an hour to get ready. Instead of putting everything back on top of the dresser Saira arranged the ornaments about the room; only the jewellery casket did she hide. There was not a lot in it, but the few pieces looked very valuable.

As she had originally intended to stay for only two nights Saira had not brought many clothes with her. The lilac spotted dress she had worn today was the nicest she had and would have to do for this evening as well.

By five to seven she was ready, her hair freshly brushed and re-plaited, a touch of grey eyeshadow, mascara, lipstick, though why she was bothering she did not know. Most of the time she never wore make-up. It had to be because she needed a boost to her morale, for she felt like a wrung-out dishcloth, at one of her lowest ebbs; she felt like marching up to Frenton Hall and throwing Jarrett's offer back in his face.

Even when she walked up his tree-lined drive Saira still had not made up her mind what her answer was going to be. All she knew was that her stomach was churning round and round, she felt like death warmed up, and she wished she'd had the nerve to pack her bags and go home.

It would be a fatal mistake to accept, she knew that, and yet still she dithered. And the trouble was she did not know whether the attraction was the cottage—or Jarrett himself! The actual thought that she could still be drawn to this man after what he had done was abhorrent—and yet it persisted! The very idea nauseated her.

Jarrett appeared on the steps before she could ring the doorbell, wearing a lightweight fawn suit, a white shirt, and a ready smile of welcome on his face, as though the whole explosive affair had never happened. 'I like a woman who's punctual,' he said.

Saira did not know how he could put such a major quarrel behind him, how he could act as though nothing had happened, how he could control himself like this—and reluctantly she had to admire him. She had no such power herself over her emotions.

'First things first,' he said as he led her inside. 'I think you ought to ring your mother. You can use the phone in the library.'

Margaret Carlton was relieved to hear from her daughter. 'I've been so worried, what's happening?'

Saira kept her news brief, not even telling her that she had found another will in Jarrett's favour, promising that she would be home tomorrow and would tell her the whole story.

When she had finished she found Jarrett in the dining-room, standing in front of a pair of tall French windows which overlooked a private walled garden.

She looked around the huge room with its pale green silk wallpaper and deeper green carpets, its mahogany Regency furniture, the long table already laid for the two of them, and could see why the cottage meant nothing to him. With all this wealth, what did one tiny little building matter? She curled her fingers into fists and her anger boiled up again.

Jarrett turned and smiled. 'Is your mother well?'

'Yes, thank you,' said Saira tightly.

He frowned, sensing her antagonism, but said nothing. 'Please, take your seat. Gibbs has supper ready for us; she won't take kindly to being kept waiting.'

She probably didn't take kindly to his guest either, thought Saira, sitting in the chair Jarrett pulled out for her. His hand rested lightly on her shoulder before he moved to his own seat, and she wished he hadn't touched her because unwanted sensations ran through her, and she felt suddenly distraught that he still had this power after all that had happened.

'When you said supper I didn't imagine anything like this,' she said, seeking a safe topic. The table was laid with white bone china edged in gold, silver cutlery, sparkling crystal glasses, pink damask napkins and a bowl of matching pink carnations as a centrepiece.

'You thought it would be a cosy meal on our laps?'

'Something like that,' she replied, though in truth she hadn't given it much thought at all. 'What are you trying to do, impress me? Show the stark contrast between your lifestyle and what I had to suffer in the cottage?'

A muscle jerked in his jaw but his voice was perfectly controlled. 'Not many girls would have stayed without the mod cons they're used to. I must say it again, Saira, you surprised me.'

'There was an issue at stake,' she declared fiercely.

'And you came through with flying colours.' His eyes were watchful on hers, almost a caress, and Saira wished she hadn't come.

It struck her that maybe his motive in being so generous was simply because he wanted an affair with her; he didn't want her to return home because he found her physically attractive; he thought he would entertain himself for a while at her expense!

If that was the case he was in for a shock. Maybe she would accept the cottage, but she certainly wouldn't be giving herself to him. There was no chance of that after what she had found out about the Armstrong-Brents.

At that point in her thoughts Mrs Gibbs came in with two bowls of steaming vegetable soup and Saira shook out her napkin and placed it on her lap. The tall woman gave her a meagre smile before turning to leave, her back ramrod-straight, her disapproval of Saira still very much in evidence.

'Why doesn't your housekeeper like me?' she asked, though she had begun to wonder whether it was because of Joy. Perhaps the woman thought she was trying to come between them.

'Mrs Gibbs has her own peculiar manner,' he told her with an easy smile. 'Just because she doesn't fawn over you, it doesn't mean to say she doesn't like you.'

Saira was not so sure. 'Whatever,' she said with a shrug, 'there's no doubt that she's an excellent cook. This is the tastiest soup I've ever had.' And to her relief their conversation during the meal was light-hearted, the chicken fricassee was delicious, and the wine went to her head. Dessert was a brandy snap basket filled with strawberries and cream which was utterly mouth-watering, and when she had finished Saira felt as though she could not eat another thing for days.

'I enjoyed that—thank you. She refolded her napkin and sat back in her chair.

'I guess it beats bread and cheese?'

Saira's eyes flashed.

He smiled. 'I think it's warm enough to have our coffee outside. Shall we?'

They sat on white cast iron chairs round a white cast iron table and a blackbird serenaded them. The sky was tinged with pink from the setting sun and the seclusion could have been heavenly—had their relationship been different! Instead Saira felt on edge as she poured their coffee from an elegantly styled silver coffee-pot. 'Cream?' she asked.

'Please.'

He waited until she had finished and he had liberally spooned sugar into his cup before saying, 'I trust you've given my offer some thought?'

So it was down to business now, thought Saira, the polite conversation over; he was expecting her answer and the trouble was she had still not made up her mind. 'Not exactly,' she admitted. 'I'm more bothered as to why you made the offer than whether I will accept.'

'You're surely still not questioning my motives?' He looked affronted. 'Isn't it sufficient that I'm doing what your aunt wanted?'

'It's too generous an offer not to have strings attached,' she replied, stirring her coffee, not looking at him, not wanting to run the risk of letting him see that he still had the power to disturb her.

All through their meal she had been aware of his presence, too much so for her peace of mind. Her body traitorously ached for him, needed him, hungered for his touch; it would not obey her commands to ignore his sensuality. But she had no intention of letting him see it; she would cloak her feelings with anger, keep him at a distance, not let him see by the merest flicker of an eyelash that he could, if he tried, have her melting in the palm of his hand.

'Oh, there are strings,' he admitted, and the familiar, intensely irritating smile curved his lips.

CHAPTER EIGHT

SAIRA'S eyes flashed as she looked at Jarrett. Damn the man, he was always so supremely confident, always so arrogantly sure of himself. 'Just as I thought,' she snapped. 'I knew it was too good to be true that you'd give me Honeysuckle Cottage out of the kindness of your heart. What are these conditions?'

Jarrett's smile widened. 'Number one, I want you to live there permanently, not use it as a holiday cottage.'

He paused for her reaction, but she said nothing and let him continue.

'Number two, I intend having it redecorated throughout and I want you to move in just as soon as it's finished. I shall put the work in hand tomorrow and don't expect it to take much longer than a week.'

Saira shook her head wildly at this last suggestion. 'I don't want anything touched.'

His brows rose. 'It needs it, Saira.'

'Then I'll do it myself,' she retorted.

'I also thought about getting central heating put in. The winter will soon be upon us and——'

'Forget it,' she broke in sharply. 'If a coal fire was good enough for Aunt Lizzie it will be good enough for me.'

He smiled suddenly and widely. 'It sounds as though you've made up your mind?'

Saira could have kicked herself. He had trapped her, he had made these suggestions knowing she would reject them and now she had virtually declared her intention of accepting his offer. She lifted her shoulders in what she hoped was an indifferent shrug. 'I'd be a fool to turn down such an offer, but you needn't look so pleased because there's one thing *I* want to make plain from the start. Once I move in the cottage will be mine, strictly mine; you will not be welcome there, understood? I want nothing more to do with you.'

He looked disconcerted by her attack, angry too, his mouth drawing into a grim, straight line. 'I hardly think that is a necessary condition.'

'Well, that's a pity, because I do,' she told him sharply. 'The only reason I'm accepting your offer is because I want to keep a bit of Aunt Lizzie in the family.'

She knew other people might have thought differently, that they wouldn't even have wanted to keep the cottage—it was a bit old-fashioned after all, and in the heart of the countryside, away from any sort of life. But she was sentimental, she had loved Lizzie dearly, and she wanted to retain something of her character. How could she do that if Jarrett Armstrong-Brent kept popping in and disconcerting her? She took great pleasure in repeating his full name to herself; it was the best way she knew of remembering what his family had done.

'You're being unreasonable,' he said brusquely. 'We'll be neighbours; we're bound to see each other from time to time.'

'In the street,' she declared. 'My home will be my own—and it's only on those conditions that I'll accept.'

She expected him to tell her to take a running jump, to declare that he had withdrawn his offer, but although he still looked angry he nodded slowly. 'If that's the way you want it.'

'It is,' she retorted.

'You drive a hard bargain, Miss Carlton.'

'A bargain, Mr Armstrong-Brent? You were the one who made the offer.' And if he agreed to let her stay under these conditions she was more strongly convinced than ever that he had some other more devious reason for wanting her here. It would be interesting to find out.

'Very well, I will not darken your door with my presence. Does that satisfy you?' The tightness of his jaw, the rigid line of his mouth, told of his displeasure all too clearly.

Saira smiled, a smile of triumph. 'That is exactly what I want. I thank you for the cottage, Mr Brent. I will go home tomorrow and come back in one week when I have sorted everything out—but I don't want the cottage touched. As from this moment it's mine, agreed?'

He inclined his head, picked up his coffee-cup and drained the contents. 'Agreed,' he said slowly, as he looked at her thoughtfully over the rim.

She picked up her cup also, sipping slowly, looking at the velvet green lawn, at the roses and honeysuckle climbing the walls of the garden, spilling their perfume into the night air. It was an incredibly peaceful and private place, considering how vast and open the rest of the grounds were. She almost felt sad that there would be no more times spent here, but she wanted to sever her relationship with Jarrett Brent completely—it was the only way she would get any peace.

He got up from his seat and came round the table to her, his face still set and serious, but holding out his hands, which she took, frowning, wondering, and let him pull her to her feet.

'Most business deals are sealed with a handshake,' he said, 'but I think we should seal ours with a kiss.' His blue eyes were intent upon hers, reading her deeply, trying to look into her soul, trying to find out exactly why she had accepted his offer.

Saira knew what he was thinking: he wanted to know whether her reasons were avaricious or emotional, whether she was interested solely in the cottage or whether *he* had something to do with it. Even though she had declared she wanted nothing more to do with him he probably thought it was all talk, that she wasn't serious, that she *couldn't* be serious. It had probably hurt his ego.

She returned his gaze, looking directly into the deep, deep blue of his eyes, trying her hardest to appear cool and indifferent. To her annoyance her senses stirred and, although she did not let her eyes waver, her whole body grew warm. 'I think a handshake is much more suitable,' she said crisply.

To her utter annoyance Jarrett smiled, one of his famous cool, controlled smiles that curved his lips but did not reach his eyes. 'Oh, no, Saira, you're not getting away that easily.'

His hand came up and took her chin, his thumb stroking, his eyes still watchful on hers, and his head came down slowly, so slowly that she could easily have escaped, but it was as though she was hypnotised. She could not move a muscle, only stand and wait for the inevitable.

The kiss triggered sensations that began with her mouth and ran down her throat and through the whole of her body, from one extremity to the other, arms and legs tingling, heart thudding, groin aching. It was all she could do to stop herself eagerly responding, to stop herself putting her arms around him, deepening the kiss, giving him the answer he expected.

But somehow, with superhuman effort, she managed it; somehow she maintained her dignity, allowing the kiss, withdrawing from it with a cool smile of her own. 'Bargain sealed,' she said primly.

Although a muscle jerked fiercely in his jaw, Jarrett managed to hold himself in check. 'Bargain sealed,' he agreed.

'And now I'd like to go back to the cottage,' she said, because if she didn't, if she remained here with him any longer, she would almost certainly give in to the very real need that was painfully surging inside her, that was making her whole body ache intolerably.

'I'll walk you back,' he announced harshly.

Saira wanted to protest, to protest strongly and loudly, but knew that she had hurt him enough, so they went together through the house, through the wide, impressive hall, out of the main door, and along the drive. The gravel scrunched beneath their feet as they walked and it was the only sound.

It was dusk now, that long velvety time between sunset and total darkness, and it was really still too early to be going home, she thought. It was not much past nine and she knew she wouldn't sleep if she went to bed—and yet what else was there to do? It was too late to think of going back to Darlington, and it would be too dark in the cottage to see to read; all she could do was sit alone with her thoughts. And what thoughts!

She had committed herself to coming back here, to living here permanently, and although she had told Jarrett he was banished from her life she somehow could not see him adhering strictly to her wishes. He had not sounded very sincere when he'd conceded. And did she want him to stay away? Her feelings were phenomenal. Not even Tony, whom she had thought at one time she would one day marry, had managed to arouse and excite her to this extent.

Out through the iron gates they went, Jarrett clanging them shut. Saira could never get over how big and impressive Frenton Hall was. 'Haven't you ever thought of selling up completely and buying somewhere smaller?' she asked, feeling a need to talk, to break this silence that put a barrier between them as hefty as a concrete wall.

Jarrett looked at her with raised eyebrows. 'Since I only bought Frenton Hall three years ago I'm hardly likely to do that. It's a listed building, an investment; part of it dates back to the seventeenth century, and I wouldn't dream of parting with it.'

'I see,' said Saira. 'I somehow got the impression that it was your family home.'

'It's going to be,' he announced proudly, 'I'd like it to stay in the Brent family for many, many years. The last of the Frentons died a few years ago after living there for generations—perhaps you knew them?'

Saira shook her head. 'No, I didn't. Do you have any brothers or sisters?'

'I have a brother in Australia,' he told her.

'And your parents?' Not that she was really concerned about William Armstrong-Brent. That man had a lot to answer for.

A cloud crossed his face. 'My mother died in a car accident six years ago and my father couldn't face life without her; he faded away. I think he died of a broken heart. They were very devoted.'

It didn't sound like the man she had met, the man who had come boldly into their house and told them they had to get out, but she could see that Jarrett was saddened—as she had been when her own father died.

They were different circumstances, though, and she still felt that if it hadn't been for William her father would have been alive now.

'So you plan to get married and begin a whole new generation of Armstrong-Brents?' Here was the opportunity to sound out Joy's theory.

'I guess that's about it,' he said with a sudden smile.

Saira felt a heaviness in the pit of her stomach. So Joy was right and he had been lying when he'd said there was nothing serious between them. He had been playing around with her, having a good time until the day came when he finally put the ring on Joy's finger and his womanising days were over. She had known it all along, but even so the thought hurt. It would have been nice had he been interested in her for her own sake.

They rounded the corner now and Honeysuckle Cottage was in view. The evening had almost come to an end. Saira's feelings were mixed. Their relationship, such as it had been, had come to an end too. It suddenly struck her that the reason she had accepted the cottage was not only because of Aunt Lizzie, not only because she wanted to preserve her memory; it was also because she wanted to be close to Jarrett!

The thought cut through her like a knife and she felt frightened, scared of the intensity of her feelings. How futile were such thoughts, such hopes, when he was promised to another woman. It was not too late to change her mind, though; she could still back out, tell him that she didn't want the cottage after all. But she didn't, she said nothing; they reached the door and she unlocked it and Jarrett said, 'You'll be all right now?'

She wanted to shake her head and say, No, I won't be all right, I want you, I want you here with me, I love you. The thought pulled her up sharp. *Did* she love

Jarrett? Was this her reason for planning to live here in
this sleepy little village that had no nightlife? Why she
was planning to cut herself off from her family and
friends? It was a heart-stopping discovery. And it
couldn't be true—could it?

Her voice was little more than a whisper. 'Yes, I'll be
fine. Thank you for this evening.'

His eyes scoured her face, as if trying to imprint her
in his memory, as if looking at her for one last time.
'Goodnight, Saira.'

'Goodnight, Jarrett.' What made her do it Saira did
not know—an impulse stronger than her mind perhaps—
but she reached up and kissed him, a quick peck, nothing
more, and it would have been all right had he not groaned
and gathered her to him. And then it was as if that one
tiny kiss unleashed pent-up passion in both of them.

They moved inside and he kicked the door shut and
his kiss demanded everything from her, draining her, exciting her, setting her on fire. There was no way she could
stop him, nor did she want to.

He swung her up in his arms, his mouth still on hers,
and carried her through to the sitting-room, and there
on the uncomfortably overstuffed sofa he let his lips drift
from hers to explore the soft skin behind her ears. Saira
had never realised before what an erogenous area this
was.

She felt herself growing more and more aroused, more
and more desperate, and when his mouth began a slow
trail down the soft skin of her throat, seeking out the
rounded curves of her breasts, she felt as though she
were spiralling to heaven. She asked no questions, she
took only what was being offered.

She made no demur when he undid the buttons on
her dress, when he pushed her bra to one side and ex-

posed her aching breasts. He touched her gently with his fingertips, oh, so gently; he looked at her, his eyes glazed with desire. 'You're so beautiful, Saira,' he muttered thickly, 'so beautiful.'

And then his mouth descended again and sweet torture filled her. Never in her wildest imaginings had she expected to feel like this. This man had magic powers, he could arouse her as no one else ever had. Oh, yes, she loved him.

He turned his attention back to her swollen breasts and time lost all meaning. She was powerless in his arms, filled with the wonder of her new-found love, taking advantage of this moment while it lasted, knowing there would not, could not, be any more.

And then the real truth of the situation hit her. She had forgotten he was a master at playing games. This meant nothing to him, nothing at all. Joy was the love of his life; she was an interlude, a minor attraction. She excited him physically—but that was all there was to it. And it must not be allowed—it must not go any further.

She put her hands on his chest and with all her strength pushed him away from her and sprang to her feet, her face showing her distaste. 'You bastard! How dare you?' She pulled her dress together and fastened it over her aching breasts. She was furious. 'I might have known that this was the reason you wanted to install me in this cottage. You thought you could have an affair with me, didn't you? You thought——'

'*Saira*!' His harsh tone, as he bounced up too, was like a slap on the face. A savage frown changed the shape of his brows, darkened his eyes. 'Are you suggesting that my motives are purely sexual?'

Her chin lifted and she eyed him with equal ferocity. 'Yes, as matter of fact. Why else would you take advantage of me like this?'

'Take advantage?' There was a sudden warning stillness about him. 'Is that what you think I was doing? Are you denying that you wanted it as much as me?'

'I suppose I can't deny it,' she flashed, 'but I'm not two-timing anyone. You don't deserve Joy.'

'Joy and I are finished.

Saira looked at him sharply. 'And I'm supposed to believe that, am I?'

'It's the truth. I told her that it's all over between us.'

'Why?'

'Because I'm not in love with her. She's known that for a long time. I'm very fond of Joy, she's a lovely girl, but I don't love her.'

'She's in love with you.'

He looked suitably guilty. 'Yes, I know.'

Saira looked at him suspiciously. 'Even if what you say is true—and I'm not sure that I believe you—you're still not welcome here.' His interest in her was superficial. They were attracted to each other for all the wrong reasons. She was even beginning to wonder whether it was love she felt for him—or were her feelings also purely physical? The thought disgusted her.

He looked hurt and angry at her harsh words and abruptly changed the subject. 'What time is your train?' he asked. 'Have you checked? Have you your ticket?'

Saira nodded. 'I picked it up on my way back from Ripon. I'm going mid-morning.'

'In that case you'll have time to come and have breakfast with me,' he said casually, 'time to get something hot inside you before your journey.'

She could not believe his audacity, not after what had just happened, and knew he was fully expecting her to refuse, so, contrarily, she inclined her head. 'Thank you, that would be nice.'

His brows lifted. She had surprised him, as she had known she would. 'I'll tell Mrs Gibbs,' he said, and then he moved to the door. 'Goodnight, Saira.'

'Goodnight, Jarrett.' She looked at him coldly and the second his back was turned she slammed the door. What a day! What an evening! What an experience! What a man! Did she really and truly love him? How could she love such a swine? She put her hands to her head and sat down again. She was so confused, so unsure of herself, so angry with herself.

Immediately she went to bed Saira fell asleep but at three in the morning she awoke and contrarily wished that Jarrett were in bed beside her. Her body grew warm at the thought of his kisses, of his hand touching her breasts, of his mouth sucking her nipples—and she never managed to get to sleep again.

At eight she walked up to the Hall, tried to ignore Mrs Gibbs' disapproving glare, greeted Jarrett coolly, and sat down with him at the table in the breakfast-room.

On the other hand his smile was warm and welcoming, and their argument last night might never have happened. It had to be an act with him. He couldn't be so impervious, so thick-skinned that their disagreement had had no effect.

She had almost chickened out, had foreseen problems in joining Jarrett again like this, knew she ought never to have agreed. She was a weak-minded fool.

As she drank her orange juice, enjoyed a bowl of muesli and tucked into crisply fried bacon, she could not help thinking how lonely it was going to be in the cottage; and although it was not too late to change her mind Saira remained silent. They discussed the weather, the day's news, everything except themselves. And when they had finished their breakfast he ran her back to the cottage where she packed her few belongings.

'When you return, all will be in order,' he said. 'You won't have to sit in the dark or eat cold meals.'

'But no decorating,' she insisted.

'If that is your wish.'

'It is.'

They were talking as though they were relative strangers, as though yesterday's intimacy had never happened, but it was best this way, Saira decided; she could handle this. Were he to touch her or kiss her, her resistance would fall away and she would be like putty in his hands. Last night she had managed to reject him, but she wouldn't always be able to do that.

'There's some of my aunt's jewellery on top of the kitchen dresser,' she said. 'I think it ought to be put into a safety deposit box.'

'I have my own safe. I'll put it there,' he told her. 'Stop worrying, Saira.'

'But I do worry. All that stuff's been sitting there for months; it could have been stolen.'

'If it will make you feel happier we'll move the most valuable things now,' he suggested. 'Although I thought I knew your aunt well, I wasn't aware that she'd got that stuff tucked away, though I'm not surprised. She was pretty eccentric at times.'

His comments interested Saira; it made her wonder yet again whether he had taken advantage of her aunt to get his hands on the cottage. Old and ill *and* eccentric! Of one thing she was certain: she would never trust him completely until she knew all the facts. They would come out eventually, if she was patient, if she waited. One day she would learn the truth.

They were quiet during the short journey to Thirsk station, each preoccupied with their own thoughts, and when Jarrett stood beside her on the platform Saira felt surprisingly sad at the thought of parting from him. In five days she had developed a love she had never expected; it almost frightened her, and it was wrong to think of going back when nothing could ever come of it, but she knew she would.

He smiled down at her as the train pulled into the station. 'Goodbye, Saira. Take care of yourself. Let me know when you're coming and I'll be here to meet you.'

She hoped he would kiss her but he didn't, he merely stood and looked at her with the usual smile that didn't reach his eyes. He was carefully, annoyingly, supremely controlled and she had no way at all of knowing what he was thinking.

'Thanks for the offer,' she said, 'but I shall be in my car; there's no need at all for you to trouble yourself about me.' Because she had contrarily wanted and expected more from him, because she was disappointed and upset, her tone was cool and impersonal.

Muscles tightened in his jaw, and his eyes were coldly blue and completely expressionless. 'This is goodbye, then.' He opened one of the doors on the train without further ado, Saira climbed in, he closed it, and in a matter of seconds the train began to move out of the station.

Saira did not look out of the window. She could not, for she didn't want Jarrett to see her tears. She did not even understand them herself. Although the situation was of her own making, and although she knew without a doubt that she had done the right thing, she still could not help feeling distraught.

It was ironic that she had fallen in love with the wrong man. And after all she had gone through with Tony! Lord, she was a fool, a complete idiot, and the best thing she could do was never return to Amplethwaite; write to Jarrett, tell him she had changed her mind, and let that be an end to it. But she knew she wouldn't. She was well and truly hooked.

The journey was too short; she had hardly begun to sort her muddled thoughts before they arrived in Darlington. She took a taxi and her mother had the door open before she could find her key, greeting her warmly and helping her carry her case inside their small semi-detached red-brick house.

Saira flopped into a brown Dralon armchair that was part of their three-piece suite, feeling utterly exhausted. It wasn't the journey, thirty miles was nothing; it was mental tiredness, the strain of thinking too much about the man she unfortunately loved.

'I'll make you a cup of tea, dear, and then you can tell me everything.' Mrs Carlton, tall, with blue-rinsed grey hair and immaculate dress sense, hurried into the kitchen. Saira closed her eyes and the next thing she knew her mother was back.

'I must have dozed,' she apologised.

'Haven't you been sleeping well?' In Margaret Carlton's book no one slept in the middle of the day; it was decadent.

'Not really. There was no electricity in the cottage and—— '

'What?' Her mother, in the companion chair, sat up straight and looked at her daughter in horror. 'No electricity? Then what on earth made you stay? Good heavens, how have you heated water? How have you bathed? Have you eaten properly?'

'I've managed, Mother,' said Saira, wishing she had said nothing; she might have known her mother would be up in arms.

'You should have come home.'

'I needed to sort things out. No way was I going to let Jarrett claim ownership of the cottage without finding proof.'

'Jarrett? You mean Mr Brent?' asked the older woman sharply.

Her first mistake! Saira had not intended letting her mother know how friendly they had become—or unfriendly, as it happened. 'Yes, of course, Mr Brent. He asked me to call him Jarrett.'

'Really?' Her mother appeared to find the thought distasteful. 'Have you seen much of him?'

'Only as much as necessary,' Saira answered.

'And did you sort matters out? This man, whoever he is, cannot possibly own Honeysuckle Cottage. It's ridiculous. There has to be some mistake. Drink your tea, Saira, before it gets cold.'

Saira obediently picked up her cup and saucer and took a sip, before setting it back down on the coffee-table. 'There's no mistake, Mother, it belongs to him all right. I found another will, one that Mr Kirby knew nothing about. It makes no mention whatsoever of the cottage, so she must have sold it.'

'But you still haven't positive proof?' persisted the older woman.

'Not exactly,' Saira agreed, 'I haven't seen the deeds, but Mr Kirby is dealing with it. He will let me know what the outcome is.'

Mrs Carlton shook her head. 'This is a most outrageous state of affairs. I think I'll go up there myself and find out what this man is playing at.'

'No, Mother,' cried Saira at once, knowing her parent would only make matters worse; and then, more calmly, 'It wouldn't help, really it wouldn't. It's all in hand.'

'I don't like to think that you're losing out. If your great-aunt wanted you to have the cottage then you should have it.'

Saira knew that she ought to tell her mother now that she was going back, that Jarrett had given it to her, but somehow she couldn't. She knew her mother; she would read too much into it, would either suspect something was going on between them, or that he was blackmailing her in some way. It was far better to say nothing. And so she just sat and listened and drank her tea, saying yes and no in all the right places.

They ate their lunch and talked some more and later, much to her surprise, Tony came to see her. The only way he could have known she was back was if her mother had told him. Mrs Carlton had always had a soft spot for Tony and had been upset when they broke up.

He came straight across the room and pulled her into his arms, kissing her soundly, and Saira was so surprised that she didn't stop him. 'Oh, Saira,' he said, 'I've missed you. I made the biggest mistake of my life when I went out with Rebecca; I love you, my darling. Please, please, will you have me back?'

CHAPTER NINE

TONY had brown eyes, black hair, a long, serious face and was almost as tall as Jarrett—but there was no comparison between the two men. Tony did not possess the same strength of character, the same charisma, or the arrogance—though that was hardly a plus point in Jarrett's favour.

Tony was looking pleadingly at Saira now, and she could never see Jarrett doing that; it was doubtful the Yorkshire man would ever admit he was wrong. There was a world of difference between them, and Saira wondered how she had ever thought herself in love with Tony.

She pulled out of his embrace and suggested he sit down on the settee beside her. Tony frowned, sensing that all was not as he would like it to be. 'You're still mad at me? I understand that, Saira, but——'

'Tony.' She put her finger to his lips, effectively silencing him. 'Please, don't go on. It's over between us. You can't put the clock back.'

He shook his head. 'I hurt you, I know. I was foolish, I let you down, I did the unforgivable—but it was a mistake. You are the one I love.' His eyes were pained, his tone pleading.

'I'm sorry, Tony,' she said, 'but I've done a lot of hard thinking since we split up. It would never have worked; we're not right for each other.'

'How can you say that?' he asked loudly. 'We were together for two years, we never had a cross word, we——'

'And then you went off with someone else,' she interjected.

He looked sad for a moment. 'What you're saying is, you can't forgive me for that?'

'What I'm saying is that it gave me the chance to think about us, to realise that what we had wasn't strong enough. It would never have survived, Tony, even if you hadn't found yourself another girlfriend.'

She hadn't thought that at the time; she had been heartbroken. But since meeting Jarrett, since falling in love with him, she had realised that what she felt for Tony had been nothing. Had they married it would never have lasted. Their relationship had been too boring; they had muddled along without any real excitement in their lives, not even in the beginning—so what basis was that for a lifetime's happiness?

He took her hands and he looked at her intently. 'Is there anyone else, Saira?'

Saira shook her head. Not for anything was she going to tell him about Jarrett nor her mother. She might love Jarrett but he felt nothing for her, nothing deep and meaningful, so there was no point in saying anything. 'There's no one else, Tony,' she said.

He looked relieved. 'Then there's still a chance?'

She grimaced. 'Tony, please, don't get your hopes up. It's all over between us, it really is. I'm fond of you still, but I don't love you enough to want to start anything again.'

'You're serious, aren't you?'

Saira nodded.

He heaved a sigh. 'I was a fool, a giant fool, and now I've lost you.'

'I'm sorry, Tony,' she whispered.

'Not half so sorry as me,' he said, and at that moment
her mother came into the room carrying a tray of tea,
and she looked pleased when she saw Tony holding her
daughter's hands. But Saira immediately pulled away
from him and moved to the other end of the settee and
the conversation turned to Honeysuckle Cottage and
Jarrett Brent's unfortunate claim on it.

Saira had still said nothing about Jarrett offering to
make her a present of the cottage, nor that she planned
to go back up there at the end of next week. It was too
soon for such revelations; there would be too many
questions asked, too much to tell.

Tomorrow she would go to work and put in her notice;
she had decided a clean break was best. Although, as
Jarrett had said, thirty miles was not too much to travel,
she still thought it would be better to find a job nearer
to Amplethwaite. She would leave a week on Friday and
go back up to Amplethwaite on the Saturday or Sunday.

She felt dreadful keeping her plans from her mother
but Saira knew how she would react, she would want to
know every intimate detail: why Jarrett had made the
offer, whether there was anything between them; if not,
it was too generous, and he had to have some ulterior
motive. Was he to be trusted? What sort of a man was
he? And so on.

And if she dared tell her mother that Jarrett was
William Armstrong-Brent's son, then her mother would
be over there straight away giving the man a piece of her
mind. And Saira didn't want this; she wanted to deal
with Jarrett herself. Maybe later she would tell her
mother, when things were sorted out when she had settled
in, when she had found out exactly what lay behind his
offer. But not now, not yet.

Finally Tony left, after declaring that he would be round to see her again, and her mother gave up on the subject of Jarrett Brent and the cottage, and at the end of the day Saira was all too glad to fall into bed.

She slept only fitfully, though, there was far too much on her mind, and the next morning her mother, upon seeing the dark shadows beneath her eyes demanded to know what was wrong.

'I guess I was overtired,' answered Saira, 'I couldn't sleep.'

'You're not worrying over the cottage?'

'Of course not.' And it was the truth.

'Then it's probably because you haven't been eating properly. Goodness, how could you survive without electricity? That man has the brains of a sparrow suggesting you live there while everything was sorted out. But never mind, I've cooked you a good breakfast. We'll have you as right as rain in no time at all.'

Saira did not feel like eating but she dutifully cleared her plate and then backed her Fiesta out of the garage and drove to work, after thanking her mother for getting it repaired while she was away.

Mr James, her employer was pleased to see her back but shocked to hear that she was going to leave them altogether, and the next few days passed incredibly slowly.

Saira found herself thinking constantly about Jarrett. He became the hub of her universe, and no matter how hard she tried to push him from her mind, she couldn't. Was he seeing Joy? she kept asking herself. Had it been all talk when he said he had finished with her completely? Would Joy let him go? Or would she fight for him?

Tony came round more often than she would have liked. He seemed to be having difficulty in taking no for an answer, and on the next Thursday he suggested they go to the cinema and perhaps to McDonald's afterwards.

It was not what Saira wanted, but since there were only another two days before she left it seemed churlish to refuse. She was unusually quiet and the evening wasn't a success, and when they were seated in McDonald's with their burger and fries in front of them he asked her what was wrong.

'I know there's no chance of us getting back together,' he said, 'I've accepted that, but there's something else, isn't there? You've not been your usual self all the week. Are you still worrying about the cottage? Are you disappointed your aunt sold?'

'Upset that she *needed* to,' insisted Saira, her tone sharp, 'and actually I'm going back there on Saturday.'

He frowned suddenly and harshly. 'What for? I thought you said your aunt's solicitor was sorting everything out. What is there to do? Do you want me to come with you? I can easily——'

'No—it's nothing like that,' she assured him at once. 'I'm—well—I'm actually moving into the cottage permanently.'

He looked at her in total disbelief, shaking his head, his brows drawn together in a frown. 'You're what?'

'I've given up my job here,' she announced. 'I'm going to live in Amplethwaite.'

'But I don't understand. The cottage isn't yours.' A growing suspicion darkened his eyes. 'It's Jarrett Brent, isn't it? This has something to do with him. You've fallen for him, haven't you? That's the reason you don't want me; you're in love with him? You lied when you said there was no one else.'

His tone had risen, many eyes were on them, and Saira could foresee a full-scale argument ensuing if she wasn't careful. She wanted to yell back at him and say that *he* had gone off with someone else, hadn't he, and she'd been expected to accept it, but instead she said quietly, 'It's nothing like that.'

'You mean to say he's letting you stay there out of the goodness of his heart?' he sneered.

'As a matter of fact, yes,' Saira answered. She did not want to make matters worse by telling him that Jarrett was making her a present of Honeysuckle Cottage. 'He was very fond of my aunt, and when he found out that she had originally wanted me to have the cottage he suggested I use it for as long as I like.'

'With no strings attached?' His tone was caustic, unusually so, and Saira knew he was deeply hurt.

'No strings,' she answered softly.

He heaved a sigh and seemed to be accepting finally that he had lost her. 'If it's to get away from me, Saira, you don't have to do it. I'll get out of your life if that's what you want.'

'It's not because of you, Tony,' she said softly, touching his arm. 'I've always loved Honeysuckle Cottage, and when Jarrett offered to let me live there I jumped at the chance.'

'Does your mother know?'

Saira shook her head.

'She won't be happy either.'

'I know.' Saira twisted her lips wryly. 'But she's another reason I want to move. I stayed with her after Father died and my sisters got married because I felt she couldn't cope on her own. But I'm doing neither of us any favours. She's fine now; it's time I fled the nest. It's time for my mother to accept that she won't have me for ever.'

He nodded, and they finished their meal, though neither enjoyed it, and he took her home; and when Saira told her mother what she planned to do the older woman was outraged. 'How can you do this to me?' she cried. Their ensuing argument carried on long into the night and, after lunch on Saturday, when Saira piled her belongings into her car, her mother wasn't speaking to her.

Saira was very distressed. She hated falling out with her mother like this, and even her new life could be fraught with problems. What if Jarrett did not keep away from her? What if she couldn't stay away from him? What if she couldn't stand the loneliness? What if, what if, what if... Saira's head ached and she stopped at a roadside café for a cup of tea and then went for a walk, and it was evening when she finally drove into Amplethwaite's narrow street.

And it wasn't until she got there that Saira realised she did not have a key to get in. She had given it back to Jarrett so that he could let the electricity board people in, and now she was stuck, she would have to go up to the Hall and announce her presence, which was the very last thing she wanted to do.

It was with some trepidation and a rapidly beating heart that she headed in its direction, leaving her red Fiesta outside the cottage. She had seen the curtains move in Mrs Edistone's house across the road and knew that her arrival had not gone unnoticed.

Saira pushed open the huge iron gates and walked the length of the long gravel drive, ringing the doorbell, and then waiting breathlessly. What would it be like seeing Jarrett again? She had missed him more than she even dared admit to herself; and yet she was still going to insist that he stay out of her life. It was the only way she would be able to live with herself. If she saw too much of him there was no way she would be able to hide her love.

When no one immediately answered the door she gave a groan. He was probably out, most people went out on a Saturday night. She ought to have telephoned, told him when she was coming and he could have left the key. Now she was stuck.

And then the door opened and it was neither Jarrett nor Mrs Gibbs who stood there, but Joy; Joy with her hair tousled and a flush to her cheeks, and Saira's worst fears were realised. So much for Jarrett declaring that their affair had ended! He had lied to her!

Suddenly she couldn't take it. Instead of calmly asking for the key to the cottage she turned tail and fled, and Jarrett, coming up behind the dark-haired girl, saw only the back of Saira's retreating body.

It was so unlike her to run away and yet she couldn't help herself. She felt humiliated somehow, as though she was making a fool of herself coming to live in the cottage when Jarrett had no real interest in her. Although no one knew of her love, it still felt as though she was declaring her innermost feelings to the whole world.

She heard Jarrett behind her. 'Saira,' he called, 'wait!' But she did not stop, and it was not until she fumbled with the latch on the gates that he caught up with her. His hand clamped on her shoulder, twisting her to face him, puzzlement in his blue eyes. 'Saira, what's wrong? Why are you running away? You should have let me know you were coming.'

'I suppose I should,' she said, 'but I forgot I didn't have a key until I got here. And now I've spoilt your

evening. I should have guessed you and Joy
would be——'

'Saira, Saira,' he cut in swiftly, 'there's not only Joy
in my house, there's a whole party. Why don't you come
and join us? We've been playing charades and it got a
bit out of hand.'

Saira was not sure that she believed him, even though
she knew that most visitors parked their cars in the big
courtyard round the other side. It was entirely feasible
that there were other people in the house; it was just that
she had looked forward eagerly to seeing him, to feasting
her eyes on his face, and then to discover he was with
Joy was like a bucket of cold water thrown over her.

'No, thank you,' she said. 'All I wanted was the key.
I'm tired, I want to go to bed, and you ought to get back
to your guests.' All the old familiar feelings returned.
She felt herself drowning in the hypnotic blue depths of
his eyes. She had wondered whether her love had been
real or imagined, and now she knew—and she also knew
that she had made a fatal mistake in coming here. There
would be no happiness, only heartache piled upon
heartache. It was a pointless, pointless thing she had
done.

'As if I want to bother with my guests now you're
here,' he growled, looking at her with so much desire in
his eyes that Saira felt herself begin to tremble.

She held out her hand. 'Give me the key.' And she
deliberately made her tone hard.

'It's in the house. I'll have to fetch it.'

'That's all right, I'll wait here.'

He was gone and back in no time, and insisted on
accompanying her, on opening the door himself,
switching on the light and entering the cottage with her.

'It's all right,' she said. 'I don't need you now.'

'But I need you, Saira,' he growled, and pulled her into his arms. 'Lord, I've missed you. I thought you were never going to come back.'

'You've missed me?' she asked coldly, pulling away from him.

'Indeed I have.'

'You mean you've missed our arguments?'

He smiled. 'If that's the way you want to put it.'

'There can be no other way,' she insisted. 'I told you before I left that I want nothing more to do with you. Go back to Joy, marry her, make babies, but keep well away from me.'

His eyes hardened, a muscle jerked in his jaw. 'If I thought you really meant that, Saira, I would withdraw my offer of the cottage.'

Saira eyed him hostilely. 'You know damn well I mean it, it was my one and only condition. But—if you've changed *your* mind, then I'll go, I'll go right now.' She was furious. He was making her feel as though she was in the wrong when all she had done was accept his offer— an offer made because he had a guilty conscience!

He shook his head. 'You've been back less than a few minutes and here we are arguing like cat and dog. I'll fetch your cases in, Saira.'

Her chin lifted in true Saira spirit. 'There's no need; I can manage myself.'

But he did; he emptied her car, took the cases upstairs, and only when he was satisfied that she would be all right did he go. In the doorway he took her face between his palms and kissed her; a gentle, friendly kiss on the forehead, nothing she could take exception to, and yet it lit fires within her and she was extremely disturbed when he had gone.

She dropped down into her great-aunt's rocking chair and wondered what the future held in store. She had let her heart rule her head, she knew that now. She had tried to tell herself that it was because she loved the cottage, but that wasn't so. She did like it, and it reminded her so much of her favourite aunt, but it wasn't solely the cottage that had made her accept Jarrett's offer.

She sat a long time with her thoughts before she made herself move. She telephoned her mother to say she had arrived safely, though her reception was distinctly frosty. She unpacked and stowed all her clothes in the capacious wardrobe, she took a bath, thinking it might be nice to get a shower installed, and then, too tired even for a bedtime drink, she slipped into bed and fell into an instant and dreamless sleep.

When she awoke on Sunday morning it took her a minute or two to remember where she was, then she smiled and stretched luxuriously. She was in her own little cottage, she was her own boss, she could do what she liked, get up when she liked, eat when she liked, go out when she liked. For the very first time in her life she was a free agent. The thought was joyous.

She sprang out of bed, washed and dressed and was just on her way downstairs when Jarrett knocked on the door. She knew it was him straight away, she could tell his distinctive knock, and she groaned inwardly, even though a contrary inner excitement slid through her veins.

She wrenched open the door and eyed him coldly. 'What do you want?' And felt devastated by the sight of him in a navy casual shirt and a pair of light blue jeans.

His thick brows rose though his smile never faded. 'Now there's a greeting, when I've come to welcome you into the village.'

'Welcome me?' she echoed.

'You don't believe me?'

She shook her head.

He lifted his shoulders. 'Very well, I've come to see whether you slept well?'

'Like a log,' she acknowledged, 'and now you've ascertained the state of my health you can go again. You seem to keep forgetting that this cottage is strictly out of bounds where you're concerned.'

'You drive a hard bargain, Miss Carlton.'

'And you're a very persistent man, Mr Brent.'

'Is that a fault?'

'It is where you're concerned,' she snapped. 'How can I get through to you that I don't want you here?'

'I'm hoping that persistence will pay off and you will change your mind.' The smile he gave her was that of a schoolboy pleading for leniency.

'Never,' she replied. 'I think you're forgetting that I have every reason in the world to hate you, but apart from that you already have a girlfriend, and don't tell me again that it's all over because I refuse to believe you. You're the world's biggest louse.'

He grinned. 'I missed your fire and brimstone, Saira.'

She stamped her foot angrily. 'This isn't funny. I'm serious.'

'And so am I serious. I do want to see you, Saira, I did miss you. May I come in?'

What could she say? Once the cottage was legally hers, once she had the deeds in her hand, then she would keep the door locked and barred, maybe even change the locks; he wouldn't set one foot inside, she would see to

that. But in the meantime... She was seething as she
stepped back into the room.

'Can I offer you a cup of coffee?' she asked ungraciously, then suddenly remembered that she hadn't
bought any groceries. 'No, forget that, I have no milk.'

He frowned. 'Did you not make yourself a drink
before you went to bed?'

'No, I was too tired.'

'Then I suggest you take a look.'

Frowning, Saira went through to the kitchen and to
her amazement both the fridge and the freezer were well
stocked, the pantry too. 'You didn't have to do this,'
she said, angry that he had taken the liberty but overcome
by his thoughtfulness. 'How much do I owe you?'

He smiled. 'I'll settle for a kiss.'

Saira shook her head, her pigtail flying, and pro-
ceeded to fill the kettle.

But she had reckoned without Jarrett's tenacity. While
her back was turned and her hands were occupied he
came up silently behind her, sliding his hands around
her waist and nuzzling and nibbling her neck.

She almost dropped the kettle, and his touch was every
bit as exciting as she remembered. She knew that she
ought to shrug him off, demand that he leave her alone,
but her sanity deserted her; it had taken only a second
for her to become a slave to her emotions.

She let him take the kettle out of her hands, she allowed him to turn her, to hold her in an embrace that
was all she had been dreaming of ever since she left here
a week ago. She looked up into deep blue eyes that held
her captive; she felt the thud of her heart and the hardening of her breasts, nipples urging against the soft
cotton of her T-shirt—and she knew without a doubt
that this was the reason she had come back.

A few moments she would allow herself, a few seconds' ecstasy, and then she would push him away from her.

But the seconds turned to minutes, mouths met in a mutually acceptable kiss, tongues entwining, passion mounting. Saira could no more have stopped him than she could have leapt over the moon. She urged her body against his, felt the rising tide of his desire, wriggled uncontrollably, animal whimpers escaping from the back of her throat.

Had Jarrett spoken it would have shattered the experience; she would have come to her senses, she would have wrenched herself away from him; but he didn't speak, he let his eyes do the talking. They were the deepest, darkest blue she had ever seen them, glazed with desire, exposing his feelings, exciting her, adding to her delirium.

When his hand touched her breast, when he rubbed the hard nub of his thumb across her nipple, her excitement increased, and when he lifted her shirt so that he could stroke her burgeoning naked skin she wanted to cry out with the sheer sweet torment of it all.

And the torture really began when he lowered his head and sucked her aching nipple into his mouth, his tongue rasping, teeth teasing. Her head fell back on her shoulders as she surrendered completely; there was the most powerful ache in the pit of her stomach, and time really did lose all meaning.

Where it would all have ended she did not know had the insistent ring of the telephone not rudely interrupted them. Jarrett swore, Saira groaned, and he suggested she not answer.

But the spell had been broken and even when it turned out to be a wrong number Saira refused to let Jarrett touch her again. 'It was a mistake, a big mistake,' she insisted.

'I don't see how it can be a mistake when you were so obviously enjoying it,' he grumbled, 'when you actively responded. Dearest, dearest Saira, you want this as much as me.'

'Don't "dearest Saira" me,' she snapped, actually more angry with herself than Jarrett. Was she insane? Had she taken leave of her senses? If she let him do this on day one, what would happen on day two and day three and day four, and for goodness knew how long? 'I didn't want it, I don't want it, I hate you.'

As usual he was completely unflustered, absolutely in control of himself, the inevitable smile curving his lips. 'Something tells me that you don't really know what you do want. I think that instead of fighting me you should let things take their course.'

'You mean have an affair with you?' she snapped, even more irritated by his calm manner. 'Because that's all you want, isn't it? I knew it was a big mistake accepting your offer; I knew this was all you wanted. God, I'm a fool.'

And the trouble was, she didn't know how she was going to get out of it. She had given herself away completely. She had let Jarrett see how easy it was to make her respond. He would use this to his advantage now.

CHAPTER TEN

'SAIRA, you're no fool.' Jarrett's deep voice was gravelly, his blue eyes watchful, his whole stance relaxed, thumbs hooked into the edge of his trouser pockets. 'You hate yourself for not having the strength of your convictions, but I don't think that's a bad thing.'

'You wouldn't, when it's to your advantage,' she retorted, her eyes flashing as she bounced from foot to foot, her anger a total contrast to Jarrett's calmness. But he was right, her anger was definitely directed more at herself than him.

It was so unlike her to lose control, she had always been in complete charge of her life, and now this man was making her go all to pieces. Lord, she hated him as much as she loved him. It was an unreal situation and she was stuck in it. She had thrown in her job, she didn't really want to go home, she liked living here in her aunt's cottage, but she did want to be left alone. How could she make him accept that?

She turned back to the kettle, plugged it in and switched it on, then she got out cups and saucers, the coffee jar and the sugar bowl and the milk from the fridge, and all the time she refused to look at him, refused to acknowledge his presence.

But he was looking at her, looking at her very, very closely, watching everything she did, every single movement she made, and her nerves grew more and more taut with every second that passed. So much so that when she turned to look at him, about to vent her wrath on

him once again, her hand caught one of the cups and it
went flying to the floor, smashing into a dozen different
pieces.

She swore violently and dropped to her knees. How
could she have been so careless? One by one she began
to pick up the pieces. Her aunt had had these china cups
for years and years; she could remember, on rare occasions, drinking out of them as a child, admiring the
colourful fruits that adorned them, touching the gold
rims, always conscious that she must be very, very careful
not to drop one. She blamed Jarrett now, she blamed
him entirely. If he hadn't turned up, if he hadn't got her
into such a state, it would never have happened.

He appeared at her side, squatting next to her, dustpan
and brush in hand, although Saira wasn't aware that he
had moved. 'Here, let me.'

She glared and wanted to order him out, but knew
that it was imperative she retain some sort of decorum,
so she stood and let him sweep up the fragments of china,
watching him as he had watched her earlier, and by the
time he had finished she had regained control of herself
and was able to finish making their coffee.

She handed his to him without a smile, making it very
clear that she still resented his presence, that he was not
welcome and never would be.

He took his cup through to the sitting-room, Saira
having no recourse but to follow, and they sat down.
Jarrett in her aunt's rocking chair, Saira on the overstuffed sofa. He still had that annoying, complacent,
confident smile on his face, and she was fuming.

'What did your mother have to say about you coming
to live here?' he asked, the delicate china cup dwarfed
by his large, capable hands. He was giving her his undivided attention and Saira found it difficult to handle.

She eyed him sharply, trying to give the impression that it was no business of his. 'She wasn't happy about it,' she replied.

'She still thinks you should live at home with her?' There was astonishment both in his voice and on his face. 'Doesn't she want you to have a life of your own? Goodness, Saira, you can't live with her for the rest of your life.'

It was the wrong thing for him to have said. It triggered off memories she would prefer to forget and she flashed him a look of pure anger. 'And whose fault is it that she's a widow?'

His mouth tightened. 'I cannot believe you're still blaming my father.' His deep blue eyes were hard upon hers.

'Who else is there to blame?' she riposted.

'No one,' he acknowledged. 'It was just one of those things. I'm sorry it happened, but you really cannot state categorically that my father was the cause of his death.'

Saira shook her head, her green eyes shooting pure hatred. 'This is one point over which you and I will never agree,' she told him coldly and angrily. 'As far as I'm concerned, William Armstrong-Brent was at fault. I won't have it any other way. And if you don't like my attitude and want to change your mind about this cottage then just say so. I'll willingly get out of here and out of your life.'

His eyes still held her captive. 'I have no wish to change my mind,' he announced tersely.

'Because you still think I'm easy game?' she snapped, playing with her plait, trying in vain to keep her temper under control.

'Why do you distrust me so, Saira?' There was a crisp coldness to his voice that went with the hardness of his eyes, and it was at times like this that Saira easily forget that she was in love with him.

'Because,' she answered coolly, 'no man makes an offer like you have without a reason—and not necessarily a good one.'

'That isn't an answer,' he clipped, his tone barely civil. And yet in contrast to her own agitated movements he was relaxed and still. 'If you mistrust me you must have a basis for it. What have I done that makes you so suspicious—apart from the fact that I bought this cottage from your aunt?'

'Isn't that enough?' she demanded loudly. Right from the beginning she had hated the thought of him duping her aunt, and once she had found out that he was William Amstrong-Brent's son it had made matters worse. He was unbelievable; he was selfish, ruthless and uncaring, thinking only of himself and what he wanted to get out of life. She hated him.

'You thought at first that I was conning you, isn't that right?' he rasped. 'You thought I didn't really own Honeysuckle Cottage, you thought I'd claimed it after your aunt died and was trying to make out it was mine.' When she failed to answer, he sprang up and, taking her by the shoulders, he shook her. 'I said, isn't that right?'

Saira winced with the sudden pain. 'Yes-s.' It was a hiss, forced out of her, and she tried to twist free but Jarrett had other ideas. She was held in a vice-like grip which would probably result in a bruise tomorrow.

'So,' he growled, 'what's wrong now? You've discovered that it is all perfectly legal and above board, so why do you still mistrust me?' The fierceness of his eyes held her captive.

She drew in a deep, angry breath. 'Because you're a hateful swine, because there are lots of things I don't like about you, because——'

'Because you don't have a very high opinion of the male sex in general, do you?' he cut in harshly, finally letting her go.

'You can say that again,' she flared, jumping to her feet, not liking his considerable advantage when he stood over her. 'I don't trust any single one of you and I'd be very grateful if you'd steer clear of this cottage in future. You're not playing the game fair considering it was one of the conditions I made.'

He lifted his shoulders, the inevitable smile quickly back in place. 'Conditions, my dear Saira, like rules, are made to be broken. You're irresistible. How can I keep away from you? How can I sit up there in my house knowing that you're here all alone?'

Unsure whether he was mocking her, she retorted angrily, 'You could consider Joy, for one thing. The moment my back was turned, you and she were together; it proves you didn't finish with her; it proves you were lying. I'm nothing more than a diversion—and I don't want to be a diversion. Why won't you consider *my* feelings?' She was so irate that she was shouting.

'How about mine?' His eyes were steady on hers, mesmerising her, recreating the sensations that had screamed through her earlier.

Saira shook her head fiercely, her eyes a vivid, brilliant green, her whole body shaking. How could she feel like this in the middle of an argument? What the hell was wrong with her? Why did she love this hateful man? 'I don't care about your feelings,' she raged. 'I just want you out of my life.'

'I'm afraid that might prove very difficult,' he said, still smiling, still supremely confident, his eyes never wavering off hers. 'When I want something I usually go all out to get it; and——' his voice became lower '—I want you, Saira.'

She could not believe his audacity. She knew what he meant all right: he wanted her in his bed! He wanted an affair! What he didn't want was a permanent relationship. Well, he could think again if he thought she was willing. She might be in love with him, but she had her pride—and pride most definitely forbade that she give herself to him.

But before she could respond, before she could say anything at all in her own defence, he smiled and said, 'I'll cook us breakfast,' and disappeared into the kitchen.

She looked after him in astonishment and asked herself why she hadn't immediately stopped him, why she hadn't said something. He was taking over, and she was letting him! Goodness, was she out of her mind? Was she going mad?

By the time she had pulled herself together sufficiently to go after him, Jarrett had the grill turned on and was expertly cutting the rind off the bacon he had earlier stocked up with, snipping the fat so that it would not curl up while it was cooking.

'Would you like the full works?' he enquired, smiling at her pleasantly.

Saira could see there was no stopping him and she lifted her shoulders. 'Just egg and bacon and perhaps a grilled tomato, if there are any,' she answered, trying to match his casual tone.

He surprised her with his proficiency and when they sat down to eat she said grudgingly, 'I thought that, having Mrs Gibbs to do everything for you, you wouldn't be able to cook.'

'My mother insisted on teaching us,' he told her. 'Brad wasn't particularly keen but I thought it was great fun. I used to dream about becoming one of the world's greatest chefs.'

'But decided to follow your father's example and throw people out of their homes instead,' she retorted acidly, 'building big new business parks and hyper-markets and making yourself lots of money.'

He stopped eating and looked at her coldly and Saira began to feel uncomfortable. She was out of order. Even though she had thought such a thing she ought not to have said it, it was unkind and unworthy. But she was not going to apologise. It was the truth whichever way you looked at it. And the fact that he didn't say any-thing made her feel worse.

They continued their meal in silence and she guessed that he would be off as soon as they had finished, which suited her. If she had achieved nothing else she would have got rid of him.

But it didn't work out like that. She actually could not believe it when he suggested they go for a drive. She looked at him in wide-eyed surprise. 'I'm serious,' he said. 'It would be a shame to waste all this summer sunshine.'

To her consternation Saira found herself finally agreeing. What else had she got to do? The cottage needed a thorough spring-clean, but she had plenty of time, she did not have to start today, and, although she had declared that she wanted nothing to do with him, it was not strictly true.

She loved this man; she wanted, more than anything, to spend all her days with him, to forget that his interest in her was purely physical. Her insistence that he keep away had been an act of self-preservation and she was no longer sure that she wanted to isolate herself from him.

'Shall we take a picnic?' she asked. 'Shall I make some sandwiches?' It was a good job he had thought to fill up her fridge.

'No, no, we'll get a meal somewhere,' he insisted, and, with a twinkle in his eye, 'let's go, now, before you change your mind.'

Jarrett drove steadily, giving her time to admire the Yorkshire countryside. Their first port of call was Kilburn, just a few miles away. He paused outside the Robert Thompson workshops and Saira saw the huge piles of maturing oak stacked outside. 'One day we'll watch the furniture being made,' he said.

'And the mice being carved?' asked Saira with interest. 'Why can't we go in now?'

'Because we'd spend too much time there and end up not getting anywhere at all,' he answered firmly. 'Have you seen the White Horse?'

'Not since I was a child,' confessed Saira, knowing instantly what he was talking about. Her aunt had told her the story many times. The horse was cut out of the hillside above Kilburn by the village schoolmaster and his pupils in the mid 1800s and had been kept white all these years by whitewash and chalk chippings. It was three hundred and fourteen feet long and two hundred and twenty-eight feet high and could be seen from many miles away. She amazed herself by remembering these figures.

He stopped the car in one of the lanes where they had an excellent view. 'Thomas Taylor will always be remembered,' Jarrett said; 'he was a great friend of one of my ancestors. To celebrate the completion of the horse two bullocks were roasted and over a hundred gallons of beer drunk.'

'Some party,' said Saira. 'What made him do it in the first place?'

'Because he'd seen the White Horse in Berkshire and he thought Roulston Scar was just made for the same sort of thing. It's certainly an eyecatcher, don't you agree?'

Saira nodded. 'It's not as big as I remember.'

'Is anything ever, once we're grown up?'

They had their lunch at Middleham-in-Coverdale, a village steeped in history but now more renowned for its many racing stables. They parked on the cobbles in the market place, enjoying a traditional ploughman's lunch in the Black Bull—rich crusty bread and huge chunks of cheese with lettuce and tomato and pickles, washed down with a half-pint of shandy. It was an unexpected sort of lunch but Saira thoroughly enjoyed it and afterwards they explored the castle ruins.

'King Richard III lived here once,' Jarrett told her, 'but his successor, Henry Tudor, let it fall into ruin and half of the town of Middleham was built from stone stolen from the castle. It's amazing anything was left,' he added, 'and yet it's reputedly still one of the most majestic and romantic ruins in the country.'

Their drive took them next through the very heart of the Yorkshire Dales, through some of the most magnificent countryside Saira had ever seen. They stopped frequently, listening to murmuring streams, admiring sweeping vistas, miles and miles of dry-stone walls, negotiating steep hairpin bends, climbing, descending, passing through sleepy hamlets, talking, laughing, enjoying. He did not overstep the mark once, he was friendly and fun but not overpowering.

Hours later they stopped for another meal, again in a pub, but this time in its restaurant where Jarrett ordered steak and Saira lemon chicken, and she felt contrarily sad that the day was drawing to a close. She felt that she had got to know Jarrett a lot better.

He had been the perfect gentleman, not putting a hand out of place, not saying a word to offend her; he had been like a big brother, teasing, daring, joking. It had been a fun day and although at all times she was aware of her attraction to Jarrett, Saira had somehow managed to push it to one side and just enjoy being with him.

It was almost ten by the time they finally got back to Honeysuckle Cottage. Considering how angry she had been when he turned up at the cottage this morning, Saira was sorry now that the day had come to an end. 'I've really enjoyed myself,' she said to Jarrett as she climbed out of his car. 'Would you like to come in for a cup of tea or coffee or something?'

'I like the idea of the "something",' he said, his eyes glinting as he unfolded himself from the car.

Saira felt a *frisson* of excitement run through her. She had to be careful. Maybe today had been all part of his devious plot, maybe he had intended to lull her into a false sense of security so that when the time came she would fall into his arms without a murmur.

They ended up drinking decaffeinated coffee in the kitchen, perched on Aunt Lizzie's white wooden stools with their dark green upholstered seats. Saira had deliberately refrained from suggesting they move into the sitting-room because she knew they would get too comfortable and all too quickly things could get out of hand. She had every intention of keeping Jarrett at arm's length for what was left of the day.

At ten-thirty she looked pointedly at her watch and yawned.

'You're ready for bed?'

Saira nodded. 'It's been a lovely day, Jarrett. I've truly enjoyed myself.'

'Good, I'm glad.' He looked at her intently, watching and seeming to be waiting for her to make the next move.

She felt her heart race and it would have been the easiest thing in the world to move into his arms, but it would be fatal. It would set a precedent, and lord knew she couldn't handle it. So instead she got up and walked through to the front door, opening it and standing back for Jarrett to leave. He looked disappointed, but, surprisingly, respected her wishes. 'Have you plans for tomorrow?' he asked.

'I'm going job-hunting,' she announced firmly. She had some savings but because she did not know how much it would cost to live here she needed to be very careful until she was working again.

'Why not enjoy a holiday first?' His eyes were persuasive on hers, and it would be so easy to change her mind, especially if he intended spending the time with her.

But she shook her head. 'It would drive me insane sitting doing nothing.'

'In that case,' he said with a mysterious smile, 'I have news for you. I asked around and an acquaintance of mine who runs a chemist's shop in Thirsk says he'll see you. He's not promising anything, but it could be worth your while.'

'Thank you, you're very kind,' said Saira. She ought to be pleased, and hated herself for feeling suspicious again. Why was he doing all these things? Why was he so keen for her to stay? There had to be some ulterior motive; he couldn't possibly be doing it out of the kindness of his heart.

The kiss he gave her was perfunctory, his lips touching her brow, his palms on her cheeks, and he looked at her long and hard, but that was all, and Saira was puzzled and disappointed. Although, contrarily, if he had tried to kiss her properly, if he had wanted to end the day making love, she would have fought him with all her might. Perhaps he knew that? Perhaps he knew her better than she thought?

She went to bed feeling thoroughly frustrated and woke hoping he would call in to see her before he went to work. Her thoughts had been full of him, all night long, and she knew he would be in her mind during the day also. But he never came and the next few days followed a similar sort of pattern.

The job hadn't materialised. Jarrett's friend had no real vacancy as the shop was small and did not warrant two pharmacists; he suggested she try one of the bigger chemists in York. But as York was as far south as Darlington was north it would have been a pointless exercise. She tried all of the local towns without success and began to wish that she had not been so hasty in giving up her job, it wouldn't have hurt her to travel each day while she was looking around.

Sometimes Jarrett took her out, but not often, and these were the occasions she looked forward to. For some reason, though, he still kept her strictly at arm's length, no more kisses, no embraces; he was the epitome of the perfect gentleman—and although she should have been happy about it, although she told herself it was what she wanted, Saira could not help feeling disappointed, peeved even. What had happened? Had he changed his mind about her? She couldn't believe that he was respecting her wishes. He hadn't before; why should he begin now?

One day, having got bored with sitting in and eating alone, Saira decided to go to the Fauconberg Arms for her evening meal. She had not seen Jarrett for days and was really fed up. When she saw his white Mercedes parked on the cobbles outside her heartbeats quickened— until it occurred to her that Coxwold was Joy's home town and he was obviously here with her. Joy was the reason she hadn't seen much of him lately!

Not even venturing inside Saira turned her car around and headed straight back home. It was wrong to feel upset, she had known all along that Jarrett and Joy were an item, had never really believed him when he had said it was all over, yet the green eye of jealousy would not go away. She hated the thought of the two of them together, of Jarrett kissing this dark-haired girl, making love to her, whispering sweet nothings, perhaps even making plans for their wedding.

Without a doubt it was her own fault. She had done too good a job of telling him that she wanted no physical contact between them. She did not even feel like eating now. She put the television on but had no idea what she was watching; she felt miserable and resentful and half wished she hadn't come to live here. It wouldn't have been so bad had she got a job, somewhere to go during the day, some other interest, other people to talk to. She had never felt so lonely.

She had already thoroughly cleaned the cottage, re-painted the kitchen and wallpapered the sitting-room. There was nothing else that needed doing, not desper-ately; everything sparkled and shone as it had in her aunt's day. She wondered now whether she was destined to live here all alone for the rest of her life—like her great-aunt.

Elizabeth had been married once, her beloved Edward dying at a very young age. She had lived on his mem-ories for over fifty years; his memories and his money. Edward had been a very wealthy man, coming from a well-to-do, aristocratic family, and she had never had financial problems. This was why Saira could not under-stand why she had sold Jarrett the cottage.

Her aunt hadn't lived here when they were first married; they'd had a fine big house in Bedale. She had moved here after she was widowed, against the wishes of his family, but feeling a need to be somewhere where there were no memories of Edward.

She had actually not been much older than Saira was now and, thinking about it, Saira could not cope with the idea of spending the rest of her life here by herself.

Jarrett came round the next evening, took one look at her unhappy face and asked what was wrong.

'What is wrong is that I can't find a job,' she snapped. And you're spending too much time with Joy! This was what was really getting at her. She loved Jarrett so much, and yet there was no hope for her. 'I hate being here by myself all day and every day; it's driving me insane.'

His lips curled. 'Poor Saira.'

'Don't make fun of me,' she retorted. It was so easy to be angry with him these days, all because she was frustrated—very much so. Her body craved his every hour they were together, every minute, every second—and he didn't even know! His lack of interest proved that he had never been serious about her, that he had been trying it on, and when it hadn't worked he had gone back to Joy.

'I hadn't counted on the fact that you would get fed up so soon,' he said. 'Country life isn't for you, is that what you're saying?'

'No,' she answered, shaking her head. Her hair was loose this evening, she had washed it earlier and it cascaded over her shoulders, flying every which way, and she tossed it back impatiently. 'I like the countryside, but I need a job, that's what's really getting me down.'

'What else can you do besides dish out medicines?' He was in her aunt's rocking chair as usual, his elbows on the arms, his fingers steepled, his chin resting lightly on them. He gave every impression of being truly interested.

Saira pulled a face. 'Not a lot. I've never really trained for anything else, except typing—I did a course in that once—but I don't have word processing skills or anything like that, and I've never worked in an office so I guess that's out.'

'Are you a good typist?'

'I'm accurate, if a little slow,' she admitted, 'and that's only because I haven't had much practice.'

He looked thoughtful for a moment and then said, 'I know someone who's in urgent need of a typist. He's writing a book—and doing it in longhand. He only has an old manual typewriter, though. Would you be interested?'

'Would I?' she asked, her face lighting up. 'I'd do anything, I'm desperate. Who is he? Where does he live? Is it far from here?' This was a bolt from the blue; she had never thought about typing. If he employed her it would be great.

'Round the corner, actually,' Jarrett informed her, smiling at the enthusiasm on her face.

Saira frowned. Where round the corner?

'At Frenton Hall.'

Then she looked suspicious. 'It's you!'

'The very same,' he agreed.

'And you're writing a book?' Her frown deepened. 'What about? You've never mentioned it before. Are you making this up, Jarrett? Are you inventing a job just to give me something to do?' And to get her into his house! Was his little waiting game nearly over? Better be careful, she told herself.

He put his head to one side. 'Would I do a thing like that?'

'I wouldn't put it past you,' she said with a wary laugh.

'It's true, as a matter of fact,' he assured her. 'I am writing a book. It's a history of the Frenton family. I came across some old diaries, and, my word, the things that happened in that family! It just has to be written.'

Saira could see that he was serious. 'And you really would trust me to type it?'

'If you're up to it, and in case you're wondering, I would pay you a proper wage. I wouldn't take advantage of you.'

'Jarrett, you're a life-saver.' Without even thinking about it, Saira got up from her chair and flung her arms around him.

It was the first proper physical contact between them in weeks and it was as if she had touched a trigger. His arms tightened around her, his eyes darkened, and there was only the slightest hesitation before his mouth came down on hers.

CHAPTER ELEVEN

As JARRETT kissed her Saira thought of Joy, and then dismissed the girl almost immediately. She did not want a guilty conscience spoiling this moment. The kiss was one of desperation, of pure basic hunger... mouths clinging, tongues entwining, bodies pressing. This was what had been missing out of her life, she thought: not the job, not the loneliness, but Jarrett!

For long, sweet seconds she surrendered herself to him. It did not matter that he belonged to another woman, it did not matter that he was the enemy, that his father had destroyed her father, that he had turned her aunt out of her cottage. Nothing mattered except that he was kissing her as though he really meant it, that she was in the arms of the man she loved, accepting his kisses, returning them, needing them, assuaging her hunger.

Even when his mouth seared a trail down the column of her throat she made no attempt to stop him, letting her head fall back, her breathing unsteady. God, she ached for him, felt as though she was bursting, as though there was so much love waiting to spill out, so much pleasure needed, so much of everything.

She held his head tightly between her hands, her fingers crooked, fingertips digging in. She arched her body, urging herself against him, feeling her heart, the whole of her, throbbing wildly and painfully.

When he stripped off her pink cotton blouse and disposed of her bra with the same indecent haste she made no attempt to stop him. The only sound that left her lips was a whimper of satisfaction as he took her nipples between thumb and forefinger. It was sweet, sweet torture. And then his tongue caressed her aching curves, his teeth nipping, his mouth sucking.

The last time they had made love like this it was the telephone that had brought her to her senses; this time there was nothing to stop them—except her pride. And through the haze of her pleasure Saira knew that if she didn't call a halt now it would be too late, much too late. She must never forget that, while his kisses meant everything to her, they meant nothing to him.

He had bided his time, he had behaved with the utmost propriety, and then suddenly, when her resistance was low, when she had began to think that she was mistaken about him, he had struck. God, he was cunning. Yet even so it took all her willpower to push him from her.

Jarrett frowned when she stepped back a pace and tried to take her again into his arms. 'Now what's wrong?' he asked. 'What have I done?'

'This is wrong. You and I are wrong,' she cried passionately, pulling her blouse back over her shoulders, folding it across herself, crossing her arms too, as if trying to shield herself from him. 'Damn you, Jarrett, why don't you keep out of my life?'

To her extreme annoyance he smiled, and his tone was softly persuasive when he spoke. 'Can a bear resist honey?'

Saira glared. 'You're talking nonsense. I don't think you find me irresistible at all; I think you find me an amusing diversion.'

'A diversion?' His brows rose with some amusement, his eyes alight.

'Yes,' she snapped, 'from Joy.'

'But I've told you, it's all over between Joy and me.'

'It didn't look like that when I came to the Fauconberg Arms the other night,' Saira rasped. 'What more proof do I need?'

'You're saying you saw me with Joy?' queried Jarrett brusquely.

'Well, not exactly,' she admitted, 'but your car was outside, and why else would you be there if it wasn't to have dinner with Joy?'

'The only time I've been in the Fauconberg recently was by myself.' His lips were suddenly tight, his nostrils dilated, angry that she should accuse him so groundlessly. 'Why did you run away without waiting to find out?'

Because I was consumed with jealousy, answered Saira silently. 'What does it matter?' she cried. 'I don't want you to touch me *ever* again. I don't even want to see you again.'

'Your protests are getting stale, Saira.'

'I don't care,' she flashed, 'I mean them.'

'Are you saying you don't want the job?'

In the heat of the moment Saira had actually forgotten and she gave an inward groan. Of course she wanted the job. 'Yes, I want it,' she said reluctantly.

'In that case there's no way you'll avoid me.' And he looked delighted.

'It will be on a strict business basis,' she insisted.

'Of course.' But he said it too easily and she was not reassured.

How she slept that night Saira didn't know; there was so much on her mind, so much to think about. After all her vows never to trust another man she had fallen deeply and irrevocably in love. What a mess she was making of her life.

It was with some trepidation that Saira went up to Frenton Hall the next morning. She fully expected Jarrett to want to take up where he had left off, and was surprised and contrarily put out when he assumed a very professional approach. He took her into his study, indicated the pile of pages he had written so far, introduced her to the ancient old typewriter, and then left her to get on with it while he went about his day's work.

For a few minutes Saira did nothing but look at the room around her. It was predominantly a brown room— beige walls, a tan leather-covered desk, a tan armchair, donkey brown carpet, and curtains that were neither green nor brown. There were pictures of horses on the walls, overflowing bookcases, filing cabinets with drawers not properly closed; it was a cluttered, much used room, homely and comfortable, and she liked it better than any other room in the house.

It was stamped indelibly with Jarrett's personality, and as she began working she could almost feel him in the room with her. His untidy black handwriting was difficult to read and the typewriter was a mean machine, but she felt confident that he would be satisfied with her typing.

At the end of the day her shoulders and neck ached from sitting bent over Jarrett's work for so long—she had taken an hour off for her lunch, going back home and eating a cheese sandwich—and now she stood and stretched, covered the typewriter and prepared to go home again, not sure whether it would be an empty evening or whether Jarrett would come to visit her.

He did not come, and the next morning he had already left for work when she arrived at the Hall. Saira was deeply disappointed. Tuesday and Wednesday followed the same pattern and it began to look as though she was not going to see very much of him at all.

She threw herself into her work and soon got used to his handwriting, and her speed improved the more she typed. It actually made fascinating reading and gave her an insight into the history of Frenton Hall.

Occasionally she saw Joy out riding and wondered whether it was with her that Jarrett spent his spare time. The thought knotted her stomach and did nothing to improve her temper. And when Joy came to see her she knew she had been right to distrust him.

'I want to know what game you're playing,' the girl said, walking rudely into Jarrett's study without even bothering to knock.

Saira was taken completely by surprise and looked at Joy wonderingly. 'Game? I'm not playing games. What are you talking about?

'For a start, what are you doing here?' The girl's eyes were hostile as she stood in front of the desk, her whole demeanour one of outrage.

'I'm doing some work for Jarrett,' Saira answered. 'I should have thought it was obvious.'

'What work?' came the sharp response.

Saira eyed the girl coldly. Even if she was a friend of Jarrett's she had no right walking in here like this. 'I don't see that it has anything to do with you.'

'Jarrett's never needed anyone to do any typing for him before,' Joy complained. 'I can type myself; if there's anything he needs urgently I could do it. Why has he asked you? And another thing, why are you still in Jarrett's cottage?'

If anything was designed to anger Saira it was this. Jarrett's cottage indeed! 'My aunt's cottage,' she corrected furiously.

'Jarrett bought it from her.' Brown eyes were hard and cold and faintly condescending.

So she knew all his business, thought Saira angrily. 'Maybe, but it's mine again now,' she rasped.

'You mean you're living here permanently?' A frown drew the girl's finely pencilled brows together; this was obviously something she had not counted on.

'That's right.' Saira eyed her challengingly.

'Jarrett sold back to you?'

Saira smiled. 'Let's say we came to an arrangement. If you want any more details you'll have to ask him.'

Joy sniffed condescendingly. 'You seem to be getting mighty pally with him, but it won't get you anywhere, I promise. I've warned you before. Jarrett and I have an understanding. It won't be long now before we get married.'

'That isn't what Jarrett told me,' said Saira, resenting the girl's high and mighty manner.

'Oh?' It was tight-lipped question.

'He said that it was all over between you; so as far as I'm concerned he's a free man—and I shall see him whenever I like,' she added defiantly.

'Jarrett might have said that,' the girl retorted, 'we did have a little tiff, but that's all forgotten now, we're back together, and I don't want you chasing after him. I'm warning you again, Saira, I won't stand for it. If you carry on seeing Jarrett you can expect something very unpleasant to happen. You might even find yourself out of a home,' she finished vehemently.

Saira's brows rose. 'I don't think that even you would have that sort of influence over Jarrett. I'm here now and I'm here to stay—and it was at his suggestion.' As on the last occasion she had come face to face with this girl, Joy aggravated her to such an extent that she was prepared to pretend there was more between them than there really was.

Joy's face flushed with anger. 'You might think you've won, for now,' she spat furiously, 'but let me tell you, you're wasting your time; Jarrett is mine, he always has been and he always will be.' She banged the door behind her as she left.

Saira was left feeling both bemused and angry. It felt as if a whirlwind had passed through Jarrett's study, and although she did not want to believe Joy when she said they were back together she found that it was easier to believe this girl than it was Jarrett himself.

She threw herself into his work with a vengeance, and on Friday Jarrett came home before she had finished for the day. 'How are you getting on?' he asked. 'I trust you didn't encounter too many problems? I'm sorry I couldn't get home; I got tied up in some business that refused to be solved.'

'You've been away all this time?' she asked, her heart beating unsteadily.

'I'm afraid so, didn't Mrs Gibbs tell you?'

Saira shook her head. She had hardly spoken two words to the woman. His housekeeper gave every impression of resenting her presence in the house.

Jarrett frowned. 'That's strange. When I telephoned to say that I wouldn't be home I asked her to inform you. I wonder why she didn't do it? I must have a word with her.'

'You could have spoken to me yourself,' said Saira, not realising how resentful she sounded.

'My sweet Saira, I was so busy, I hardly had time for one phone call. It's been a hectic week, but I'm back now, and more than pleased to see you.' He attempted to take her into his arms but Saira backed away and he frowned. 'Aren't you pleased to see me?'

Hell, yes she was, but she wanted more from him than he was offering, and if she couldn't have all of him then she wanted nothing. After Joy's visit she had made up her mind that she was not going to let him play with her emotions any longer.

'Has something happened while I've been away?' He looked confused.

'You can say that again,' she snapped. 'Apart from the fact that you were lying when you declared it was all over between you and Joy——'

'But, Saira, it——' he began with a frown.

She went on as though he had not spoken, 'I shall never completely trust you; it's best we maintain our distance. I phoned Mr Kirby, and he's still sorting out probate on my aunt's will—and do you know what? It galls me that any of this happened. It's all your fault for tricking her out of her home.' Her eyes flashed a brilliant green and every part of her rejected him.

He took off his jacket and slung it over the back of a chair and moved towards her, trying to take her hands, but she stepped still further away from him. 'I think it's time I told you the truth,' he said quietly, his eyes surprisingly sad. 'I had hoped that as you got to know me you would accept that I would never do anything detrimental to your aunt's well-being, but as this hasn't happened, then——'

Saira looked at him sharply. 'Don't give me that rubbish.'

'You still think I drove her out of her home?' It was his turn to sound angry, not only to sound it but look it as well. His brow was as dark as a thundercloud.

'Can there possibly be any other explanation?' she scoffed. There was nothing he could say that would make her think differently.

'Sit down, Saira,' he suggested. 'This may take some time.'

She did not see how owning up to such a dirty trick could take long, but she sat nevertheless, her eyes condemning him even before he had spoken.

'Lizzie was increasingly feeling the effect of our cold, damp winters; what with bronchitis and one thing and another she decided to go and spend a few months with her friends in Florida. Every year they asked her and always she refused.'

'I know that,' said Saira sharply. 'You're not telling me anything new.'

He went on, 'Then you also know that while she was out there she was taken gravely ill?'

Saira nodded, although her aunt, when she had telephoned to say she was back, had typically made very light of it.

'Her medical costs vastly outstripped her standard medical insurance—so I offered to pay them.'

Saira frowned. '*You* offered to pay?' This didn't go with the image she had formed of him. 'Why? Aunt Lizzie had money of her own. Why should you pay?'

'Your aunt did have money,' he said, 'but she lost a lot on the stock market; she wasn't as well off as she led everyone to believe. I offered to pay because I loved Lizzie. She was like a grandmother and a mother all rolled into one. But your aunt, being the type of person she was, would not accept charity and insisted I accept the cottage in return.'

Saira looked at him sharply, not wanting to believe him, but feeling that it was too fanciful a tale to be a lie. And it sounded like the sort of thing her aunt would do. She'd been an independent, stubborn old woman, never liking to be beholden to anyone.

'Were you going to let her carry on living here?'

'Naturally.' He looked affronted that she could think otherwise. 'Until the end of her days. I didn't really want the cottage, I only took it to make her happy.'

'Then why didn't you tell me this in the beginning? Why didn't you produce the deeds? Why did you keep prevaricating?' Saira was thoroughly confused.

His smile was deep and warm. 'My sweet, from the very first moment I saw you I was hooked. I was intrigued by this fiery stranger; I was bowled over. I had to think up a way to keep you close so that I could get to know you better.'

'You mean all that stuff about not being able to find them was just a ploy to keep me here?' she asked incredulously.

He inclined his head. 'Guilty as accused.'

Saira began to laugh. 'I don't believe this. I'd got you down as being devious and cunning, but never for this reason. Are you truly saying that you were attracted to me right from the beginning?'

'Indeed I was, Saira.' He pulled her closer to him and kissed her soundly, and she wanted to ask him about Joy and what his feelings for her were but there wasn't time because all of a sudden the door burst open and Joy herself came rushing into the room.

'Jarrett, thank goodness you're back. Pegg's ill, you must come to her. I've called the vet but he hasn't arrived yet and I'm so worried.'

The tiny girl in her jodhpurs and neat-fitting shirt was almost tugging at his arm. She had scarcely looked at

Saira, though she couldn't have failed to notice the embrace she had disturbed.

Jarrett was all at once serious and attentive and with the briefest, 'Excuse me,' he strode from the room, Joy running after him.

Saira stood a moment. It had all happened so quickly. One second Jarrett was kissing her, declaring his love, the next he was hurrying out with the girl who had professed she was going to marry him. And he had gone so easily; without, it seemed, a moment's regret that they had been disturbed. She tried to tell herself that it was because he was concerned for the horse, that it had nothing to do with Joy, but the errant thought would not go away.

She picked up her bag and prepared to go home and then at the last moment decided to go to the stables herself and see what was wrong with Pegg. Joy had sounded so worried, it must be something very serious.

But as she reached the stables all Saira saw was Joy in Jarrett's arms, her small pointed face reaching up for his kiss, and, feeling sickened and disappointed, she fled.

How right she had been to distrust him. What a swine he was, what a two-timing bastard! Let him try to tell her again that he loved her. She could see it now for the ploy it was. Fed up with getting nowhere with her, he had changed his tactics, believing that once she thought he loved her she would let down her defensive barrier.

So incensed was Saira that she did not even go back to the cottage. She couldn't have rested, couldn't have sat and relaxed without thinking of Jarrett and his despicable behaviour. Instead she went to the Challoner's Arms, ordered herself a double Campari and soda and sat there drinking it and fuming and deciding what her next tactic would be.

He had made it all sound very good when he'd declared he had paid for her aunt's operation; he had really done a big job trying to get her on to his side, and it had almost worked—in fact it probably would have worked if Joy hadn't come barging in. Had the girl known she would find them in a clinch? Had it all been planned? Was the mare not sick? Was it a ruse?

Whatever the case, did it matter? The truth was that Jarrett had wasted no time in going from her arms to Joy's. He really must have thought he'd got the best of both worlds. Two women lusting after him, his choice of either. God, she felt sick.

She finished her drink and ordered another and then realised that this was no answer and walked out without touching it. But she didn't go home; she didn't want to run the risk of bumping into Jarrett again, hearing his convincing excuses. She went for a walk and did not return to the cottage until it was dark.

When a shadowy shape emerged from the side of the house Saira almost jumped out of her skin. 'Where the devil have you been?' growled Jarrett.

She eyed him coldly and distastefully. 'What does it matter to you?'

'It matters a great deal,' he rasped. 'I've been out of my mind with worry.'

'In the arms of Joy Woodstock?' she riposted, pushing open the door, snapping on the light, and stepping inside.

Jarrett followed and his face was grim and pale as he gripped her arms, shaking her, impaling her with eyes that were hurt and angry. 'In Joy's arms? Hell, Saira, you're letting your imagination run riot.'

'You're saying your mare wasn't ill?'

'I'm not saying that at all, though she wasn't as sick as Joy implied.'

'I bet she wasn't,' cried Saira. 'Not so sick that you couldn't kiss Joy the instant you thought you were safely hidden in the stables.

'You saw?'

She felt his start of surprise. 'Yes, I saw,' she snapped, trying unsuccessfully to free herself.

He groaned and let her go. 'It wasn't what it looked like.'

'Isn't that what they all say?' she countered. 'How could it have been anything else?'

'Joy rigged the whole thing,' he said, his face screwed up with pain. 'It was her last-ditch attempt to win me back. But it failed, Saira. I didn't kiss her. I held her to calm her because she seemed so worried, but when I discovered it wasn't Pegg who was on her mind but me I let her go. If you'd stayed around long enough you would have seen.'

'How can I believe you?' she asked contemptuously.

'I'll fetch Joy and make her tell you the truth,' he said firmly. 'It was also Joy who withheld the message that I would be away all the week. Mrs Gibbs asked her to tell you and she very conveniently forgot. I love you, Saira. I promise you it's all over between me and Joy.'

He looked so worried, and sounded so sincere, that Saira knew she had to believe him. 'That won't be necessary,' she said quietly. Such a scene would be far too humiliating, both for Joy and herself.

'Then you believe me?'

Silently she nodded. 'I think so.'

'Oh, Saira.' He groaned and gathered her to him again and this time she did not resist. 'It really is the truth. It was over between Joy and me the moment I set eyes on you. The trouble was she wouldn't accept it. Joy has had ⟨...⟩ts set on me since I moved here, and to begin with I was flattered—until I realised that it wasn't so much me but the lifestyle I could give her that she was interested in most.

'Foolishly, I didn't end it all there and then, and she's actually worked very hard at making herself indispensable—and then you came on the scene. She wasn't happy about that and I'm sorry if she's given you a hard time.'

'Has she accepted now that it's all over?'

Jarrett nodded. 'I didn't want to hurt her but in the end I had to be brutal. My dearest Saira, please, don't let's talk about Joy any more. I want to talk about us. I love you so much, my dearest; do you think you could learn to love me in time?'

'Oh, Jarrett.' All Saira's misgivings faded and she looked into his eyes and her whole face spoke a thousand words. 'I do love you, I've loved you for ages, and trying not to let you see it has been the most difficult thing I've ever had to do.'

He looked disbelieving, then amazed, and finally delighted. He swung her up into his arms and twirled her around, then he kissed her, and she kissed him, and time lost all meaning, and when finally they floated back down to earth she still had another question she wanted to ask before finally and completely giving herself to him.

'I believe you when you say that my aunt insisted you have her cottage,' she said, 'but how about all those other properties you've supposedly bought in the village?' She could not get out of her mind what his father had done, what she thought he was doing also.

'Dearest, doubting, Saira,' he said, shaking his head, but he was smiling also and was not hurt by her suspicions. 'The whole village once belonged to the

Frentons—as you probably discovered when you were typing my book?'

Saira nodded.

'Because of mounting debts, Rupert Frenton—the last of the line—sold most of the properties off over the years. I thought it would be nice to buy them back again as they came on the market. Not,' he added quickly, 'from a mercenary point of view. I paid well over the market value, I charge very fair rents, and repairs are always done promptly. I wanted to try to keep a village atmosphere; I wanted to stop other developers from spoiling Amplethwaite. Does that answer your question?'

Saira nodded, grimacing ruefully. 'I feel awful now. I'm sorry, I should have known what a good, kind, considerate man you are. I should never have doubted you.'

'I guess I asked for it,' he said, 'withholding those deeds the way I did. And then there's what my father did. I hope, Saira, that you're not going to hold that against me for ever?'

She shook her head. 'No. Lord knows I was incensed at the time, but you're right, your father wasn't completely to blame. I guess my father's heart attack could have happened at any time.'

'So everything's all right now?' he asked, his voice deep and sexy. 'You've no more doubts, no more suspicions, no more worries?'

'None at all,' she said, smiling up at him. What a dear, dear man he was, and how very wrong she had been to mistrust him.

'You're sure?'

'I'm sure,' she agreed.

'I have one more question to ask you.'

He looked so serious that Saira felt a little qualm of unease.

'Will you marry me, my darling Saira?'

Relief washed over her and a brilliant smile illuminated her face. 'I will.'

'Tomorrow?'

She laughed. 'As soon as you like, Jarrett. As soon as you like.'

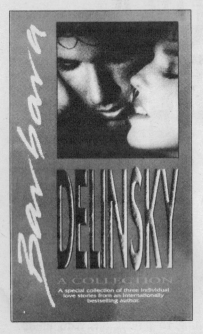

NORA ROBERTS

◆

SWEET REVENGE

Adrianne's glittering lifestyle was the perfect foil for her extraordinary talents — no one knew her as *The Shadow*, the most notorious jewel thief of the decade. She had a secret ambition to carry out the ultimate heist — one that would even an old and bitter score. But she would need all her stealth and cunning to pull it off, with Philip Chamberlain, Interpol's toughest and smartest cop, hot on her trail. His only mistake was to fall under Adrianne's seductive spell.

AVAILABLE NOW   **PRICE £4.99**

WORLDWIDE

Next Month's Romances

Each month you can choose from a wide variety of romance with Mills & Boon. Below are the new titles to look out for next month, why not ask either Mills & Boon Reader Service or your Newsagent to reserve you a copy of the titles you want to buy — just tick the titles you would like and either post to Reader Service or take it to any Newsagent and ask them to order your books.

Please save me the following titles: Please tick

		✓
A VERY STYLISH AFFAIR	Emma Darcy	
ELEMENT OF RISK	Robyn Donald	
TO HAVE AND TO HOLD	Sally Wentworth	
BURDEN OF INNOCENCE	Patricia Wilson	
LOVERS NOT FRIENDS	Helen Brooks	
THREADS OF DESTINY	Sara Wood	
INNOCENT DECEIVER	Lilian Peake	
WHISPER OF SCANDAL	Kathryn Ross	
CALYPSO'S ENCHANTMENT	Kate Walker	
SAVING THE DEVIL	Sophie Weston	
BETWEEN TWO LOVES	Rosemary Hammond	
DREAM MAN	Quinn Wilder	
STEP IN THE DARK	Marjorie Lewty	
LOVESTORM	Jennifer Taylor	
DECEPTIVE DESIRE	Sally Carr	
A PASSIONATE DECEIT	Kate Proctor	

If you would like to order these books in addition to your regular subscription from Mills & Boon Reader Service please send £1.90 per title to: Mills & Boon Reader Service, Freepost, P.O. Box 236, Croydon, Surrey, CR9 9EL, quote your Subscriber No:.................................... (if applicable) and complete the name and address details below. Alternatively, these books are available from many local Newsagents including W H Smith, J Menzies, Martins and other paperback stockists from 9 December 1994.

Name:...

Address:...

....Post Code:...........................

To Retailer: If you would like to stock M&B books please contact your regular book/magazine wholesaler for details.

You may be mailed with offers from other reputable companies as a result of this application. If you would rather not take advantage of these opportunities please tick box. ☐